The

CW00848172

The Hood's Army trilogy

Earth Invaded
Slaveworld
The Liberators

NATHAN ELLIOTT

Hood's Army
The Liberators

DRAGON
GRAFTON BOOKS
A Division of the Collins Publishing Group

LONDON GLASGOW
TORONTO SYDNEY AUCKLAND

Dragon
Grafton Books
A Division of the Collins Publishing Group
8 Grafton Street, London W1X 3LA

Published by Dragon Books 1986

First published in Great Britain in hardback by
Grafton Books 1986

Copyright © Nathan Elliott 1986

ISBN 0-583-30842-2

Printed and bound in Great Britain by
Collins, Glasgow

Set in Times

All rights reserved. No part of this publication
may be reproduced, stored in a retrieval system,
or transmitted, in any form, or by any means,
electronic, mechanical, photocopying, recording or
otherwise, without the prior permission of
the publishers.

This book is sold subject to the condition that
it shall not, by way of trade or otherwise, be
lent, re-sold, hired out or otherwise circulated
without the publisher's prior consent in any
form of binding or cover other than that
in which it is published and without a similar
condition including this condition being
imposed on the subsequent purchaser.

*For the other Nathan Elliott
and his mum, Maureen.
Two terrific people.*

1

Hood was leading his unit down a narrow valley when they were ambushed. It was sunset, and suddenly a horde of shining figures began pouring over the hillsides on both flanks of the unit. These were the alien K'Thraa – dark, squat figures inside shimmering golden auras.

'Take cover!' Hood yelled to his troops. Everyone dived behind the boulders which littered the dry valley floor.

The K'Thraa advanced down the hillsides, bluish energy bolts flashing from the barrels of the stubguns which they carried. A woman trooper, too slow in finding cover, was hit and fell face-down in the dusty earth.

Beside Hood, Marianne clipped a fresh magazine of darts into her needle-gun. Nearby, Hood's lieutenants, Big Mac and Will Redman, were doing likewise. The golden glows surrounding the aliens were force-shields which protected them from energy weapons such as laser-rifles. But they were no defence against the darts from the needle-guns.

'Fire at will!' Hood shouted to his troops.

Silver darts began flashing through the twilight as the Free Forces of Earth opened fire, and the leading K'Thraa stormtroopers started falling. But there were hordes of them, whereas Hood's unit numbered only fifty.

Hood unclipped a golden egg from his belt and

pulled out the pin. The egg was a sonic grenade, and Hood tossed it high in the air towards the K'Thraa. The grenade exploded silently, but a cluster of K'Thraa immediately fell, victims of high-frequency sound to which humans were immune. But the other aliens were quick to clamber over their bodies and continue the advance.

The rest of Hood's unit began hurling grenades, and within minutes both hillsides were strewn with dead K'Thraa. But still the aliens came. Hood was helping Marianne pull a jammed magazine from the stock of her pistol when suddenly an alien stormtrooper loomed over a boulder and fired. They were both hit at point-blank range and died instantly, their bodies slumping to the ground.

Big Mac, a tall, red-bearded Irishman, raced forward and shot down the K'Thraa with his needle-gun. Meanwhile Will Redman, in a scarlet coat and black three-cornered hat, was shouting orders to the surviving troops. Now that Hood and Marianne were dead, he and Mac were in charge of the unit.

The K'Thraa had almost breached the defensive circle of the human troops, but frantic needle-gun fire and clusters of sonic grenades had forced them back at the last moment. Darkness was falling rapidly now that the sun had set, and the glowing figures of the aliens were easy targets. Within a matter of minutes they had all been cut down.

An eerie silence abruply fell over the battlefield. Big Mac crawled around the circle of boulders, counting the troops who remained.

He crouched beside Will Redman, who was peering out through a gap between two boulders. Shining bodies littered the valley sides.

'We've lost thirty men and women,' he whispered.

Redman nodded. 'Any wounded?'

'Five. But they're all still fit to fight. I'm thinking we should get out of here right now.'

'I reckon you're right,' Will agreed. 'We need a better defensive position in case there's any more K'Thraa around.'

Mac rose to his full, towering height of well over six feet.

'All right,' he shouted to the other troops, 'we're moving out!'

The unit gathered into a cluster and emerged from the defensive circle of boulders. They began to move towards the broad end of the valley, a hundred metres ahead.

Then, without warning, the second attack began.

From both sides of the valley erupted salvoes of pale blue energy bolts. The unit stood no chance. Caught in an intense crossfire, they fell like ninepins. Big Mac was among the first to be hit, and Will Redman never reached the cover of a boulder which he darted for. He was hit in the back and died without a sound.

Seconds later, the massacre was complete. K'Thraa troopers began to shuffle forward down the hillsides to ensure that no humans remained alive. None wore force-shields, and their bloated grey bodies could scarcely be seen under the dark sky.

Suddenly the entire scene was flooded with light . . .

Half of the hall was a lecture theatre, holding stepped ranks of seats which rose almost to the ceiling. The other half contained the 'valley' in which Hood and his unit had fought their last battle.

As the lights came on, the hillsides and boulders dissolved, as did the dark sky and the K'Thraa troopers. All that remained was Hood and his soldiers, who lay on a padded floor where they had been cut down during the fighting.

The seats in the theatre were filled with cadets – young men and women who were undergoing training for the Free Forces of Earth. They had been watching an animated hologram, featuring three-dimensional images of landscape and alien attackers which had no solid reality. The images were computer-generated, and dissolved at the flick of a switch. Only Hood and his unit were real.

Hood now rose and faced his audience, as did the rest of his fallen soldiers. Under their olive-and-green tunics they wore a lining which was sensitive to beams of light and which told them when they had been 'hit' by a K'Thraa energy beam. If hit in an arm or leg, they were 'wounded' and had to behave as if injured; if hit in the body, they had been trained to 'die' as realistically as possible.

'All right,' Hood said to the cadets. 'What went wrong?'

There was a murmuring from the seats, but no one spoke out immediately. The cadets were all in their teens, and they had been under intensive training for the past six months.

'You shouldn't have gone into the valley in the first place,' one of the older cadets offered.

'Possibly,' Hood replied. 'But let's assume that it was essential we did."

'You should have sent scouts ahead to check it

8

out,' another cadet said, 'before the whole unit went in.'

Hood nodded. 'Good. Remember that: it's essential to have proper reconnaissance in combat situations. Never commit all your troops until you're certain of the strength of the enemy. Find out as much about them as you can beforehand.'

'What if there's no time?' said another voice. 'What if your scouts have been killed and you suddenly walk into a trap?'

The voice belonged to a smiling, gap-toothed teenage boy whom Hood knew well. His name was Mitch Miller, and he had helped Hood and his lieutenants escape from K'Thraa-conquered Earth a year previously.

'Good point,' Hood said, nothing in his voice betraying the fact that he knew Mitch; it was important not to show favouritism. 'Often, in real battles, there's no time to do much planning beforehand. You have to learn to react to the situation instantly. You need to be quick-thinking, but at the same time you have to try to *think ahead*. If you're attacked, it's not enough to hold off the enemy. You've either got to turn defence into attack, or find some way of making an orderly retreat so that you can regroup with the minimum of losses. So what else went wrong?'

'You got yourself killed,' said a Chinese girl.

Laughter rippled along the ranks of seats, and Hood smiled.

'So I did – and through my own carelessness. When Marianne's pistol jammed, I should have concentrated on defending her with my own weapon

9

rather than leaving us both unarmed while we tried to un-jam it. Pretty stupid, eh?'

Heads nodded around the theatre, many of the cadets suspecting that Hood had deliberately staged the incident as an example of bad soldiering.

'Still,' he went on, 'the others managed to fight the K'Thraa off, didn't they? The defensive circle was still intact. How many aliens do you reckon were killed?'

'Two hundred,' said a black cadet. All of the Earth's races were represented in the theatre.

'Not bad,' said Hood. 'We actually had three hundred aliens – *in force-shields* – and all of those were killed. So how come none of the unit got out of the valley alive?'

'There were more K'Thraa in hiding,' said a cadet.

'They weren't just in hiding – they had their force-shields turned off so that they couldn't be seen in the darkness. That's the big mistake Will and Mac made. They're both experienced soldiers, and they should never have assumed that all the aliens were dead. The K'Thraa know we carry needle-guns to penetrate their force-shields, and we may well encounter stormtroopers who aren't using them. Will and Mac should have taken that into account before they decided to move out. And because of their carelessness, the whole unit was massacred.'

Hood was silent for a moment, staring around the theatre as if to ensure that this lesson had sunk in with the cadets. He did not notice the faces of Big Mac and Will Redman, both of whom looked angry and upset.

'*Never take anything for granted with the K'Thraa,*' Hood told the cadets. 'We know that they're a

10

devious race, and you'll need to have your wits about you every second when we begin the liberation of Earth.' He paused again, then said, 'All right, that's it for today.'

As the cadets began to rise from their seats, Hood strode out of the hall, a door opening like the petals of a flower in front of him. He stepped on to an escalator which carried him rapidly upwards past tiny portholes which looked out on a swirling mass of orange-red cloud. Under his feet he could feel the gentle throb of the gravity-generators. He and thousands of other exiled humans were aboard the Worldship – a massive circular craft which was hidden at the centre of Jupiter's Red Spot.

Hood stepped off the escalator and walked down a long metal corridor, past workshops where men and women were labouring to equip his army. The K'Thraa had invaded Earth without warning two years previously, and since then Hood had escaped from Earth twice to continue his campaign of resistance. He was only twenty-one, but he already had vast experience of fighting the aliens. As military commander of the Free Forces of Earth, he was determined to launch his fleet of starships against the K'Thraa as soon as possible.

An elevator took Hood swiftly upwards to Chief Minister Leon's War Office. Leon was seated at his desk, dressed in a blue-and-white tunic. His tawny hair was swept back from his forehead, and a thick beard covered his face. At his neck he wore a silver star-medallion, the symbol of his office. Before the K'Thraa invasion, Leon had been head of the United Nations Council – the world government on Earth.

Now he was the Supreme Commander of the forces aboard the Worldship.

'Hood,' Leon said, rising from his seat. 'How's the training going?'

'Pretty well,' Hood told him. 'The cadets are eager to join the fleet, and they're quick to learn.'

'Good, good.' Leon was grinning. 'Come over here – I've got something to show you.'

He led Hood over to the broad porthole which looked out on Jupiter's murky atmosphere. A wide ramp protruded from the Worldship below the porthole, and on it sat a starship painted silver and blue.

'My new flagship,' Leon said proudly. 'It's finished at last.'

The flagship was designed like a five-pointed star, each cylindrical point converging on the central bridge where the ship's controls were located. It bristled with energy cannon and other weaponry.

'It looks good,' Hood said appreciatively.

'Good?' said Leon. 'It's magnificent!'

'What are you going to call it?'

'*Free Earth*,' Leon said without hesitation. 'It's fast, Hood. Almost as fast as *The White Swan*.'

Hood nodded, staring out at the other ramps on which starships sat. Leon's *Free Earth* was the only ship to have been built from scratch at the Worldship. The rest had been stolen from the K'Thraa during space raids over the past two years and converted for human use. Mostly they were huge rectangular craft, now painted blue and white. But one was a lustrous vessel which shone like a pearl in the Worldship's lights and was shaped like a long-necked bird on the wing. This was Hood's own battlecruiser, *The White Swan*, which he had stolen

12

from under the nose of the K'Thraa emperor himself.

The White Swan was faster and more manoeuvrable than any other starship, and it was also well-defended with weapons and a hull armoured against energy-cannon fire. Since his first escape from Earth, Hood had used the battlecruiser to capture dozens of alien starships in space. It had taken him across the gulfs of interstellar space to the K'Thraa homeworld, a planet destroyed by war. It had carried him away from Earth during his second escape from the planet a year previously. And soon, he hoped, it would lead the fleet that would liberate his planet from the invaders.

'We've captured two more starships in the past week,' Hood told Leon. 'That brings the total strength of our fleet up to a hundred and twenty. When are we going to set a date for our attack?'

'Not yet,' Leon said. 'The K'Thraa have at least ten times as many starships. We need to build up our strength more.'

'There may not be time. Every day that passes, more human slaves on Earth are dying under the aliens' control. We have to move as soon as we can.'

Leon regarded him from under his bushy eyebrows. 'I know you're impatient to attack, Hood. We're *all* impatient. But if we rush in there before we're ready, we would just be massacred. And that wouldn't do the captive population on Earth any good, would it?'

'The K'Thraa may be building up the strength of their fleet while we're doing the same.'

'There's no evidence of that.'

13

'Perhaps not. But it's getting harder to hijack starships in space. The K'Thraa are making sure that most of them are guarded by posses of interceptors to scare us off.'

Interceptors were smaller, heavily-armed craft which could travel swiftly through space and harry larger starships.

Leon walked away from the porthole and crossed to his desk. He stared at the photograph on the wall above it – a photograph of the planet Earth seen from space.

'We're just not ready yet,' he insisted. 'We owe it to everyone on Earth to make sure that when we *do* attack, we stand a chance of winning.'

'And how long is that going to take?'

Leon turned, a trace of anger in his face. 'Don't push me, Hood. You're our best general, but patience isn't a virtue of yours. I've got a council meeting with my advisers tomorrow morning, and I'll make sure your point of view is expressed. In the meantime I suggest that you concentrate on ensuring that all your troops are prepared for battle – whenever that may be.'

Hood knew he was being mildly rebuked. Normally he was quite happy to accept Leon's advice and guidance since the Chief Minister was highly respected as a wise and able politician. But in recent weeks he had found it difficult to restrain his eagerness to launch the Worldship's fleet against Earth.

'I think you're wrong,' he told Leon bluntly. 'We should attack as soon as possible. You're making a big mistake.'

Then he turned and stormed out of the War Office.

2

'We call it the MIP,' Professor Fitzwalter told Hood, indicating the device on the laboratory worktop which looked like an ordinary typewriter keyboard.

'MIP?' said Hood. 'What does that mean?'

'It's short for Multiple Image Processor. Watch.'

Wires trailed from the keyboard to an object at the other end of the worktop which looked like a black shoe box. The professor tapped a few keys, and suddenly there were five black boxes where there had only been one.

The professor went over to the five boxes and touched each in turn. His hand passed completely through four of them, only the original box proving to be solid.

'The MIP allows us to generate up to nine holo-images of an object,' the professor explained. 'It duplicates the original image down to the finest detail. They're just mirages, of course, but if you didn't know otherwise, you'd assume they were real.'

Hood's mind was already racing, and the professor was grinning at him, as if he anticipated what Hood was going to say. Chief scientist aboard the Worldship, the professor was also Marianne's father and hence – since Hood and Marianne were married – Hood's father-in-law.

'How big can you make these MIPs?' Hood was asking.

'We can install them in starships, if that's what you're asking.'

'And they'll generate multiple images of the ship?'

The professor nodded. 'Up to nine, as I said.'

'That's great news. We've got a hundred and twenty ships, but if we install one of those devices in every ship, we could increase the apparent size of our fleet . . .'

'Tenfold, if you include the originals.'

Hood smiled at the professor. 'How long will it take to build all the devices we need and then fit them into each ship?'

'We started a production line this morning, and we've got teams of engineers ready to begin installing them as soon as they're available. Assuming there are no hitches, we could have all the ships ready within a few days.'

Hood was amazed. 'This is all your own work?'

'It was a team effort, Hood.' The professor indicated the other scientists and technicians who were at work elsewhere in the large laboratory complex. 'Dozens of us were involved in the project, and I'm just the figurehead.'

'Rubbish. I bet it was your idea in the first place.'

'That's true. But I'd still be tinkering with dodgy prototypes if I'd tried to go it alone.'

There was a cautionary note in the professor's voice, as though he was stressing the value of teamwork in a more general sense for Hood's benefit. But Hood was intent on the MIP.

'I'd like one of these in *The White Swan* as soon as possible,' he said.

After a second's hesitation, the professor said,

'You'll get priority – as long as you promise not to do anything rash.'

'Me?' said Hood, pretending innocence. 'I wouldn't dream of it.'

Hood had gone to the research complex immediately after leaving Leon's War Office to check on the work being done there. The development of the Multiple Image Processor pleased him greatly. It would prove a potent means of deceiving the K'Thraa.

'There's even better news,' the professor told him. 'AMOS has come up with a devastating method for attacking the K'Thraa on Earth without any one of us having to set foot on the planet.'

'You're kidding.'

'I assure you I'm not. But you'd better hear it from him.'

The professor led Hood through the maze of open-plan laboratories and workshops which formed the research complex. He was a tall, well-built figure, his dark hair shot through with grey. He always reminded Hood more of an outdoors-man, such as a lumberjack, rather than the academic which he was.

Here and there a few laboratories were completely enclosed from the rest of the complex. One had a KEEP OUT sign in large red lettering on its door. The professor opened the door without ceremony.

The laboratory inside was small, and reams of computer print-outs littered the floor. On the far wall was a screen showing an image of the Earth as seen from space. It differed from the photograph in Leon's War Office in that a giant reddish honeycomb hung in space close by. The image came from a spy-probe in orbit near Earth, and the honeycomb was a huge solar mirror which the K'Thraa had built soon after completing their conquest of Earth.

At the centre of the room was a large, egg-shaped figure which hovered on a cushion of air. Flexible metal arms extended from his silver-and-gold banded body, and inside the clear dome which formed his head were two artificial eyes – eyes that were focused on a print-out in his square golden hands.

This was the Automated Motive Operating System, known to everyone as AMOS.

'What is it now?' the robot said irritably without looking up from the print-out. 'All I've had today is interruptions, interruptions. Can't any of you read the sign on the door? It is in English and not in hieroglyphics.'

'It's us, AMOS,' the professor said gently.

AMOS looked up, and recognition registered on his artificial face. He had been built by the professor and designed to express a variety of emotions.

'Ah,' he said, gliding forward. 'Do forgive me. I have been engaged in some rather detailed mathematical analysis which requires total concentration, but all day people have been dropping in to ask my advice on various problems. How are you both? Well, I hope.'

'We're fine,' the professor told him. 'Hood's come to hear about your latest discovery.'

'I have made five since breakfast. I'm afraid you'll have to be more specific.'

'The really important discovery, AMOS. About the mirror.'

'Ah, yes, the mirror. Well, it's simply stated. I've discovered a means of reversing the heat-concentration mechanism so that it generates cold instead.'

Hood stared at him, disbelieving. The K'Thraa home planet was a warmer world than Earth, and the aliens therefore functioned better at slightly higher temperatures. They had invaded Earth to colonize it as a replacement for their own ravaged world, and the solar mirror had been installed in orbit to concentrate the sun's heat and raise the overall surface temperature of the planet.

Hood knew well that the K'Thraa were far more sluggish at lower temperatures. All the aliens they had captured to date had soon entered a trance which led swiftly to death; but post-mortems of their bodies indicated that they were ill-equipped to survive for long at temperatures close to zero.

'A pulsed burst of short-wave radiation would do the trick just nicely,' AMOS told him. 'It would reverse the polarity of the heat-concentrating device immediately. Within an hour or two, temperatures would drop sharply.'

'Does Leon know about this?' Hood asked.

'It is only twelve hours since I discovered the precise frequency of the radiation and the exact pattern of the pulse required. I shall be presenting my findings to him before tomorrow's council meeting.'

'This is terrific news, AMOS. It means we can strike at the K'Thraa on Earth *before* we tackle their fleet in space. When could it be done?'

'Immediately, if necessary. It would require a starship to travel within a range of one million kilometres of the mirror, target on it, then transmit the signal. The mirror would immediately go into reverse.'

'But couldn't the K'Thraa then reverse it back?'

'Not with the signal I've devised. It would effectively jam the mirror so that it could only generate cold.'

'But what's to stop the K'Thraa from then destroying the mirror?'

'Nothing at all. But it would take at least an hour to do so, and by then the temperature switch would be irreversible. At present the Earth has an abnormally high overall surface temperature, and it will react violently against this if given the chance.'

Hood was trying to think of every possible flaw. 'But wouldn't we then be in danger of plunging the Earth into an Ice Age?'

AMOS swivelled his head back and forth in its metal socket.

'When the K'Thraa put the solar mirror into orbit, they also installed compensator devices at the North and South Poles. These were designed to prevent the ice-caps from melting with the increase in temperature and also to dampen down violent storms which might be caused by the heating up of the planet. If these devices are left intact, they will prevent the temperatures from dropping too low and reduce the strength of any storms. Of course, it will be uncomfortably cold for the K'Thraa.'

Hood glanced at the professor. 'It sounds perfect.'

'Its a major weapon,' the professor agreed. 'But it's something we should only use at the last minute, when our fleet is closing on Earth.'

'Yes,' said Hood, and he thought, *We must move soon*!

3

When Hood returned to his private quarters, Marianne was taking a shower. It was late, and Hood had had a busy day. He slumped on the bed, kicking off his boots.

Presently Marianne emerged, a bath towel wrapped around her.

'Guess what?' Hood said. 'Your father and AMOS have been doing some sterling work.' He proceeded to tell her about the Multiple Image Processor and AMOS's polarity reverser.

Marianne sat down at a small dressing table and started to brush her long black hair. She listened silently, without expression, and when he had finished she simply gave a small nod and said, 'That's very good.'

'Good? It's great. They're major weapons, Marianne. There's nothing stopping us from attacking Earth as soon as possible, if only Leon would give us the go-ahead.'

She said nothing to this, and at last he sensed her subdued mood.

'Is something wrong?' he asked.

She turned to look at him. 'You humiliated Will and Mac in the lecture theatre today, Hood.'

'What?'

'You made them look foolish when you told the cadets that the unit had been massacred because of their carelessness.'

21

'It was true. What did you expect me to say? We're fighting a war, and it's important that the cadets receive the best training possible. And if that means bruising a few people's dignity, then I'm afraid that's their hard luck.'

'Did it ever occur to you that Will and Mac may have deliberately made that error as a demonstration, just as you did when my needle-gun jammed?'

'They didn't say anything to me about it being a deliberate error.'

'You didn't ask them, did you? You didn't give them a chance to explain. You simply announced that they'd made a big mistake.'

Hood couldn't understand why she was making such a fuss about the matter. 'Will and Mac know me. They wouldn't take offence.'

'You didn't see their faces. You were too busy hurrying off to your next important meeting.'

'So what are you saying? Did they actually stage the error or not?'

'Yes. They both assured me they had.'

'OK, then I'll apologize to them when I see them next. Will that satisfy you?'

'No, Hood, it won't. It isn't just that particular incident. You've been like this for months now, ever since our last mission to Earth. You've changed.'

'What do you mean?'

'You just don't take into account the advice and feelings of your friends like you used to.'

'That's not true.'

'It is, and it started when we were last on Earth. You made all the decisions about what we were going to do, and the rest of us weren't consulted.'

Hood had begun to feel angry with what he felt was her unfair criticism. 'I don't expect you to wait for me to ask you for advice. I expect you to offer your own suggestions.'

'We did, Hood. When we were on Earth, we did.'

'I don't remember that. I had to make all the running.'

'That's because you've stopped listening to us. You just didn't hear. You're so determined to be in charge all the time.'

She donned a nightgown and climbed into bed.

'I'm trying to run an efficient army,' Hood said to her. 'I can't go pussyfooting around everyone. We need discipline and a vigorous leadership.'

'Will and Mac have been with you from the start, and they've saved both our lives on more than one occasion. They're your *friends*, Hood, as well as your lieutenants. You ought to show them more consideration.'

Hood sat up, turning his back to her. 'If people don't like the way I'm running things, then they can tell me face-to-face.'

'Nobody doubts your abilities, Hood. But lately you've been so concerned with liberating Earth that you've got no time for anything else – even your friends.'

'I don't want to discuss it further.'

A silence fell. Hood rose and went into the bathroom. He splashed cold water on his face, then briskly towelled his cheeks. When he emerged, he found that Marianne had switched off the main lights, leaving only a stick-lamp glowing beside the bed.

He sat down in a contour chair and picked up a

report on K'Thraa starship movements. As the chair moulded itself around him, he turned on a table-lamp and opened the report.

'It's late,' Marianne whispered. 'Come to bed.'

'I want to read this first.'

Marianne did not bother to argue; she simply turned over and closed her eyes.

Hood did his best to concentrate on the report, but he was tired and the print began to swim before his eyes. He knew he was being unreasonable towards Marianne, but her criticisms had stung him. And to some extent she was right. Since the last mission to Earth, he *had* been impatient to launch a liberation fleet. He was pouring all his energies into the task of ensuring that his army would be in the peak of fighting fettle. Because of this it was inevitable that he had less time to spend with his friends. Why couldn't Marianne understand that?

She was sleeping peacefully now, looking beautifully serene. Hood stifled a yawn, and returned his attention to the report. His head was fuzzy, thick with sleep, but he was determined to read it through before he went to bed . . .

His parents loomed out of a mist, coming towards him with smiles on their faces. They looked exactly as they had done before the K'Thraa invasion – fit and bright-eyed. They opened their arms as he hurried towards them.

Then suddenly their whole appearances changed – they became haggard and unkempt, their clothing in tatters. As he reached them he saw the agony on their faces, but just as quickly this expression gave way to looks of rage and hatred.

'You killed us!' they screamed. 'You killed your own parents!'

Then they burst into flames before his eyes.

Hood awoke with a start. He was still sitting in the contour chair, the report open in his lap. The disturbing images of the dream quickly faded, but it was not so easy to shake off the sense of shock he felt.

'Hood?' came Marianne's voice from the bed. 'Are you all right? You cried out.'

'It was just a dream,' he told her.

'Come to bed.'

Hood undressed and put on a long nightshirt. At his neck he wore a silver chain with a metallic purple stone at its centre.

He climbed into bed, still unnerved by the dream. His parents were dead, and it was indeed he who had killed them. They had been captured by the K'Thraa and imprisoned in the alien emperor's palace. Hood had been forced to destroy the palace, knowing that his parents were inside it, to prevent K'Thraa scientists from completing a research programme that endangered the survival of the Free Forces of Earth.

It was a terrible decision, but he had sacrificed his parents because he knew that they were doomed to die a lingering death in captivity anyway. But the guilt of this act had never left him, and his parents still haunted him in his dreams. It was also why, he realized, he was so eager to begin the liberation of Earth. Until the planet was free again, he would not be able to forget the heartbreaking thing he had done.

'What are you thinking?' Marianne asked abruptly.

'It's nothing,' he told her.

'Was it the same nightmare?'

He nodded.

'I wish you'd talk about it. It would help.'

He had never actually told her what the nightmare was, only that he kept dreaming it.

'It's nothing,' he insisted. 'Switch off the stick-lamp.'

He knew she was staring at him, but he did not look at her. Presently she switched off the lamp.

Hood lay there in the darkness, his eyes open. He was tired, but sleep would not come. He kept thinking of his parents, and he felt both sorrow and rage – sorrow that he had lost them, rage against the aliens who had shattered Earth's tranquillity with their invasion.

Time passed, and still Hood remained awake. Marianne was breathing gently beside him in sleep, and all was silent. The Worldship kept a twenty-four hour clock, and the digital display beside the bed told him that it was three a.m. – the depths of the night.

Suddenly Hood began to feel a warm spot against his chest. Instinctively his hand closed around the purple stone.

The stone grew warmer by the second, and Hood sensed the faintest of whispers in the air. He closed his eyes and concentrated.

Hood, came a voice in his mind.

Sha'Rani, he responded immediately, thinking the word rather than speaking it.

The voice was that of a female K'Thraa whom

26

Hood had befriended when he had last been on Earth. It was she who had given him the purple thoughtstone which he wore around his neck. The stone enabled him to communicate telepathically with Sha'Rani over great distances and without the need for the translator devices which the aliens normally wore.

I have little time, Sha'Rani said, *so we must be brief. Ro'Sharok has learned where your Worldship is hidden.*

What?

He is assembling a great fleet to send against you so that you will be destroyed.

Hood could not believe it. The Worldship was well hidden in the Great Red Spot, and there was no one on Earth – not even Sha'Rani – who knew where it was. Archmaster Ro'Sharok, the K'Thraa emperor, had to be bluffing.

He can't know, Hood said. *It must be a ruse.*

He claims that the Worldship is hidden in the atmosphere of your largest planet, at the centre of a great oval high-pressure weather system.

Which was exactly what the Great Red Spot was.

How did he find this out? Hood asked.

I do not know. But a fleet will be ready within several days, and Ro'Sharok is determined that no humans will escape alive. You must flee and find a new hiding place.

We can't. We're . . .

Hood was about to say that they were preparing their own invasion, but it was better that Sha'Rani did not know this, even though her sympathies were with the humans. She and the other female K'Thraa opposed the ruthless breeding programme which

27

turned alien children into warriors or slaves. She also wished for the Earth to be returned to human control and a new planet found for K'Thraa settlement by peaceful means.

Someone is coming, she said abruptly, *so I must break contact. Flee to safety now, while you can.*

Suddenly she was gone.

The thoughtstone slowly cooled to room temperature in Hood's hand. He stared down at it, thinking furiously. How had the K'Thraa managed to discover their hiding place? They were well hidden inside the Great Red Spot, and no K'Thraa ships had been seen in its vicinity. When his own ships went on reconnaissance flights, they had orders to return to the Worldship only when the Spot faced away from Earth and so was hidden by the bulk of Jupiter.

He had no time to worry about it now. What mattered was what they were going to do about it. They had to move quickly, otherwise all would be lost.

'Hood,' Marianne said out of the darkness, 'was that Sha'Rani?'

'Yes,' he replied. 'It's bad news, Marianne. We're going to have some unwelcome visitors.'

4

The council hall was a large room with a big oval table at its centre. Around the table sat the twelve women and men who were Leon's chief advisers. Hood burst in on them unexpectedly at the start of their meeting.

'What is the meaning of this?' said a plump man called Gorwalden, who was a stickler for correct behaviour.

'I've got some important news,' Hood announced. 'We have to launch the invasion as soon as possible.'

A tall silver-haired woman named Selen smiled. 'That sounds more like a statement than news.'

'Ro'Sharok has located the Worldship. He's preparing to launch a fleet against it in the next few days.'

For a moment there was silence around the table. Then Gorwalden spoke up: 'How can you possibly know this?'

'I know, believe me.'

Hood gave Leon a glance, and his right hand touched the thoughtstone under his uniform. This was enough to let Leon know that he had received a message from Sha'Rani. The existence of the mental link through the stone was a closely guarded secret, and for security reasons no other member of the inner council had been told about it.

'This is preposterous,' Gorwalden blustered. 'We

all know that you can't wait to invade Earth, but if you expect us to believe this cock-and-bull story – '

'Let him speak,' said Selen.

'I can't tell you how I know,' Hood said, 'but believe me, Ro'Sharok plans to send a K'Thraa fleet to Jupiter as soon as possible. We've got to take action now.'

Leon rose from his seat.

'You must excuse us for a moment,' he said to the others around the table. Then he walked towards a side door, indicating that Hood should follow him.

The door led into a small side room which was empty. Leon closed the door behind Hood and immediately said, 'Are you sure about this?'

Hood nodded. 'Sha'Rani contacted me last night. Somehow Ro'Sharok's found out that the Worldship is hiding in the Great Red Spot. He plans to destroy us here.'

'How did he find out?'

'Sha'Rani didn't know. There wasn't much time for her to talk to me. I've got a feeling she's being watched. Maybe Ro'Sharok suspects her of being in contact with us.'

'How soon did she say his fleet would be setting off?'

'She said it would be ready in several days.'

'Several? How many exactly?'

'I didn't have time to ask her. But it could be as few as three or four days. I doubt that it'll be more than a week. There's no alternative now – we have to fight.'

Leon stroked his beard, pondering.

'Has the professor told you about the Multiple Image Processor?' Hood asked. 'And about

AMOS's idea for reversing the polarity of the K'Thraa solar mirror?'

Leon nodded. 'I saw them both earlier. I was planning to announce both discoveries to the council this morning.'

'Then I suggest you do it now. It may tip the scales in persuading them that we have to launch our own fleet as soon as possible.'

They returned to the main hall, where a heated argument had obviously been taking place amongst the council members. Both Selen and Gorwalden were on their feet. Selen was an attractive woman in her thirties who had been born in Lunar City on the Moon, but raised on Earth. She had been aboard the Worldship on a survey of the Solar System when the K'Thraa invaded Earth. Gorwalden was the former Governor of Antarctica, and it was rumoured that he had fled into space as soon as the invasion began.

'I am able to assure you,' Leon said to the councillors, 'that Hood's information about Ro'Sharok's plans is utterly reliable. And if a K'Thraa fleet is to be launched against us, then urgent action must be taken to defend ourselves.'

'Then I suggest that we get out of here straight-away,' Gorwalden said. 'We simply move the Worldship to another part of Jupiter's atmosphere.'

Leon shook his head. 'Now that the K'Thraa know we're here, they'd track us down through the clouds wherever we went.'

'Then we move to another planet entirely. Take the Worldship further out to Saturn or Uranus or Neptune.'

'The Worldship hasn't got warp-jump capability,'

said Hood, 'so that would take weeks. We'd be sitting ducks out there in interplanetary space when the K'Thraa fleet arrived.'

Gorwalden looked annoyed.

'May I remind you,' he said to Hood, 'that this is a policy meeting, and that as military commander you are here in an unofficial capacity. If you wish to – '

'Nuts to that,' said Hood. 'None of us can afford to stand on ceremony when all our lives are at stake – and the lives of everyone enslaved by the K'Thraa on Earth.'

'He's right,' said Selen. 'This matter has to be decided upon now.'

'We can't possibly launch our fleet against the K'Thraa,' Gorwalden insisted. 'It's not large enough yet.'

'It could take years to build it up to a strength that would match the K'Thraa's,' Hood said. 'In the meantime, people are dying like flies on Earth.'

Gorwalden pointed a pudgy finger at Hood. 'You are a rash young man who has no respect for his elders. I will tell you now that I opposed your appointment as military commander on the grounds of inexperience. I see no reason to change my opinion.'

'If it was left to you,' Hood countered, 'we'd never make *any* move against the K'Thraa. We'd simply sit here and rot – '

'Gentlemen,' Leon said firmly, 'let's conduct this debate on a civilized basis. And before we go any further, I think it's important that we're all aware of exactly what weaponry we can deploy against the K'Thraa.'

Leon pressed a button on the console in front of him, and a door blossomed open at the far end of the hall. In walked Professor Fitzwalter, with AMOS gliding beside him.

The professor was carrying the Multiple Image Processor unit, and he set it down on the table with the black box.

'What's that?' Gorwalden immediately wanted to know.

'That,' said Hood, 'is a way of making the K'Thraa think our fleet is ten times larger than it really is.'

The professor repeated the demonstration which Hood had witnessed, the black box multiplying by five on the table at the tapping of the keyboard. Further tapping increased the number of holo-images to seven, and then to nine.

The inner council were suitably impressed, especially when the professor informed them that larger-scale units were already in production and could be installed in a starship in a matter of hours.

'The whole fleet can be fitted with the MIP units in a few days if we work flat out,' the professor told the council.

Gorwalden passed his hand through one of the images.

'They're just fakes,' he said, 'with no solid substance.'

'True,' the professor replied. 'But even if the K'Thraa eventually discover that we are generating multiple ghost images of a single ship, they would have no immediate means of knowing which is the real one, for all will register on their radar screens. It will give our fleet a decided advantage in any space battles.'

33

AMOS now explained about his scheme to reverse the polarity of the K'Thraa solar mirror.

'It would be possible to encode the precise signal required to reverse the heat-generator into each starship in our fleet without any of the crew having to know its exact pattern and frequency. This would be a useful security precaution against possible sabotage.'

'Sabotage?' said a disbelieving Gorwalden. 'What are you suggesting?'

AMOS did not immediately reply, so Gorwalden went on: 'Are you implying that any one of our crews might decide to turn traitor? If so, that is a disgraceful accusation.'

AMOS was unruffled. 'I gather that Ro'Sharok has discovered where we are hiding. Since no one on Earth is privy to this information, it strongly suggests that someone here must have informed him.'

Hood had contacted the professor and AMOS earlier that morning to let them know about the message from Sha'Rani. He himself had not considered the idea of a traitor, but AMOS's reasoning made perfect sense.

'Is this possible?' Selen asked the professor.

'I'm afraid it is,' Fitzwalter told her. 'We can't be certain, of course, but I can't think of any other way in which Ro'Sharok could have found out where we are.'

'Which only makes it more imperative that we act swiftly,' Leon said. 'I think Hood's right. We have to ready our fleet and try to head off Ro'Sharok's ships. We have to wrest the initiative from them.'

There was general agreement to this among the

inner council, only Gorwalden being resistant to the idea.

'Our spy-probes will tell us when Ro'Sharok's fleet is launched,' Leon said. 'As soon as we know it's on its way, I propose that we send our own fleet to engage it in battle.'

'What if it's launched tomorrow?' Gorwalden said. 'None of our ships will be ready.'

'We'll just have to hope that Ro'Sharok waits a few days. If you can think of a better alternative, I'd be most happy to hear it. If not, we'll take a vote on the plan.'

Gorwalden frowned and scowled, but he had nothing to offer.

'This is foolhardy,' he grumbled. 'We'll be sending lambs to the slaughter.'

'Our crews are hardly lambs,' Selen said with one of her dry smiles. 'They're as well trained as any K'Thraa.'

'And don't forget,' Hood said, 'we still have the advantage of being able to jump in and out of warp-space in seconds if we wish. The K'Thraa can't do that without first sealing themselves in protective pods, and that takes time. It gives us a great advantage in being able to out manoeuvre them.'

'You'll need it,' Gorwalden said bitterly.

'We're not asking you to fly with us,' Hood replied. 'You can stay here in safety.'

Gorwalden rose from his seat, his face red with anger. 'I resent the implication that I'm afraid to fight!'

'I didn't say that. But you have no experience of flying spacecraft, so you've got no right to criticize the quality of our fleet.'

'Quality has nothing to do with it. They may be the finest pilots and gunners in the universe, but the fact is that they're going to be heavily outnumbered. It will be a suicide mission!'

5

For the next two days, Hood was frantically busy ensuring that his crews were battle-ready and that the MIPs were being installed in his starships as swiftly as possible. On Professor Fitzwalter's advice, he decided not to activate the unit in *The White Swan* unless it was absolutely vital. The battlecruiser was like no other starship in the fleet, and the K'Thraa knew this. But if they saw ten of them flying through space they might realize sooner rather than later that they were being hoodwinked with holo-replicas. This also applied to Leon's flagship. They had to preserve as much surprise as they could.

That evening, Hood sought out Big Mac and Will Redman, whom he had not seen since the battle-simulation. Will and Mac had always been part of his crew, along with Marianne and AMOS. He wanted to be sure that both were fully prepared for immediate take-off should they receive news that Ro'Sharok's fleet had taken off.

Hood found his two lieutenants in one of the combat rooms, taking pot shots at holographic K'Thraa who kept appearing from every direction in the simulated streets of a ruined city. With them was Mitch Miller, whom Mac had taken under his wing after their last escape from Earth.

As Hood entered the combat room, a K'Thraa stormtrooper suddenly appeared in the shattered window of a building. Mitch sprang out of a doorway

37

and fired his needle-gun. The dart hit the alien in the chest, and he slumped dead across the window ledge. Mitch stood there in the street, a satisfied smile on his face.

'Good shooting,' said Mac, who was hidden behind a pile of rubble nearby. 'But you shouldn't have broken cover. Look.'

Mac was pointing to a building opposite, and there was another K'Thraa in the upper window. The alien fired, hitting Mitch in the midriff.

'Bang, bang, you're dead,' said the voice of Will Redman from inside the shell of a burnt-out hover-car. He shot down the second alien.

Mitch made a realistic show of 'dying', even though the energy bolt was nothing more than a beam of light. The solid holograms of the aliens were similarly primed to 'die' when hit by a needle-gun dart.

Mac walked over to him. 'Your aim was good, but your tactics were terrible. Why expose yourself in broad daylight when you could have stayed hidden and shot down that nasty without him even seeing you?'

Mitch sat up. 'I didn't think,' he said.

'Well, make sure you do in future. Your life may depend on it.'

The three of them had not noticed Hood, who was still standing in the doorway, half-hidden behind the image of a low brick wall.

'That's enough for today,' Mac said. '*Switch off*!'

He said the last two words loudly, and the holographic scene immediately dissolved to leave a bare room. The computer which generated the image was voice-activated.

The others now noticed Hood, and he stepped forward.

'I'm impressed,' he said to Mitch. 'Done any energy-cannon firing practice as well? We could use you on *The White Swan*.'

Hood's plan was that every ship in the fleet would carry at least one cadet, who would complete his or her training under real battle conditions. But Mitch did not reply to his question; he simply glanced awkwardly at Mac.

There was silence, and only now did Hood register that both Mac and Will looked rather uncomfortable.

'What's wrong?' he asked them.

'Nothing's wrong,' Mac replied.

But Hood knew better. 'What is it? Do you think my plan's a bad one?'

'We thought it was fine,' Will said, 'When we eventually heard about it.'

'I've been busy, so I didn't have a chance to tell you myself. I want you to be ready for take-off at the shortest notice. *The White Swan*'s going to be leading the attack.'

'We won't be flying in *The White Swan*,' Will said.

'What?'

'We asked Leon for gunnery positions aboard the *Free Earth*,' Mac told him. 'He was pleased to have us.'

Hood could scarcely believe it. 'Why?'

'We reckoned you could manage without us,' Mac said. 'You might do better with a fresh crew, us being a bit slapdash and careless, like you told the cadets.'

Hood had intended to apologize to both men for

his mistake, but now he felt only anger. 'So that's it – I've hurt your pride and so you go running to Leon.'

'We didn't run,' Will said, just as angrily. 'We couldn't see the point of working under someone who doesn't respect our abilities any more.'

'That's ridiculous.'

'So you say,' replied Mac, 'but you've had no call to ask for our advice of late, whereas Leon told us he'd be delighted to have experienced men around him. He even offered us our own ship, but we'd just as soon serve under him.'

Hood felt as if he had been slapped in the face.

'I see,' he said icily. 'And if I order you to join my crew?'

'You are our commander,' Mac said with dignity. 'If you order us, then we will not disobey you – providing that Leon also agrees.'

But Hood knew that his pride would not allow him to force men to work under him.

'Suit yourself,' he said. 'I'll find my own crew!'

Then he stalked out.

Hood took the elevator up to the research complex. He felt betrayed by Will and Mac's desertion of him, and he would not accept that he was to blame. They had simply been too sensitive and had failed to take into account the heavy responsibilities which he was carrying on his shoulders. Well, he would manage without them.

The complex was a hive of activity when he arrived, with teams of scientists and technicians frantically engaged on last-minute work to improve the fighting capability of the fleet. They were testing

40

spacesuit jet-packs; fitting night-seeing visors to helmets; giving anti-matter torpedoes a final check; assembling large MIP units before they were sent to the engineering bays to be installed in starships.

Men and women in white coats and denim coveralls were everywhere, but there was no sign of Professor Fitzwalter or AMOS. Hood guessed that the professor would be working on one of his pet projects – developing a warp-drive powerful enough to propel the Worldship through hyperspace. So far he had not yet managed to perfect such a drive, though he had told Hood that it was only a matter of time.

Hood went directly to AMOS's laboratory, where the familiar DO NOT DISTURB sign hung on the door. Inside he found AMOS tinkering with a complex device which resembled nothing more than a metal pineapple about twice his own size. The professor was sitting in a corner of the laboratory, poring over a computer print-out.

'What's that thing?' Hood asked of the pineapple.

The professor glanced up, looking rather distracted.

'Another secret weapon,' he said. 'Except that we can't get it to work properly.'

'Patience and determination is all that's required,' AMOS said confidently. 'I'm sure the device is sound in its basic construction. We simply have to – how do you humans put it? – iron out the bugs. A quaint expression, don't you think?'

'Hood,' said the professor, 'have you had any further contact from Sha'Rani?'

'No. Why?'

The professor indicated the print-out he had been

41

studying. 'We appear to have received a coded message from someone on Earth.'

'What does it say?'

'I haven't managed to decode it yet. AMOS is going to take a look at it as soon as he has the time.'

'Time is something we may be short of,' said Hood. 'I take it, AMOS, that you'll be available as a crew member for *The White Swan* when we need you.'

'Not if I haven't finished my work here. I'm afraid it must take precedence.'

Suddenly Hood felt as if he was being let down all over again. AMOS indicated the pineapple. 'This device may prove vital to our war effort. It is essential that I get it working properly.'

'And we need to decode this message,' the professor added. 'It might contain important information.'

But Hood was hardly listening to them. He felt resentful, convinced that all his closest colleagues were abandoning him when he needed them most. He did not even bother to ask what the device was; he simply walked out.

He arrived back at his quarters to find that Marianne had just returned from training a group of cadets in zero-gravity manoeuvres.

'Will and Mac are flying with Leon in the *Free Earth*,' he told her immediately, 'and AMOS is staying here to work on some invention with your father. What about you? Have you decided that you don't want to fly with me as well?'

'Of course I'll be flying with you.'

'Great,' Hood said without enthusiasm. 'At least

42

there'll be someone I know on board. We're going to need three new gunners.'

'You can't blame Will and Mac, Hood. Just lately you've been treating them as if they didn't exist.'

Suddenly the visiphone started bleeping. Hood picked up the receiver from its cradle, and the screen lit up.

It was Leon. Even before the Chief Minister spoke, Hood guessed what he was going to say:

'The K'Thraa fleet's about to be launched.'

6

Half an hour later, Hood addressed the assembled pilots and crew members in a hall near one of the docking bays. A large screen behind him showed spy-probe pictures of the K'Thraa fleet rising slowly from Earth. They looked like a swarm of angry black insects against the cloud-swirled planetscape.

'We're going to intercept the fleet as soon as possible,' Hood told his audience, 'and as close to the Earth as we can. Immediately this briefing is over, we take off. You all know what's required of you, and I'm confident that you won't let me down. We're going to blast those ships out of the sky!'

The crews cheered, and there was real passion in their cries. But there were far fewer of them in the hall than Hood had hoped. Only thirty starships were ready for take off, and it would be several hours before the rest of the fleet were fully equipped with MIP units. But several hours might be too late, and so Hood was taking out an advance force to hold the K'Thraa off. A pilot sitting at the front of the hall was quick to ask the question which Hood had been dreading:

'How many ships are there in the K'Thraa fleet?'

'Four hundred,' Hood told him.

This news was received in silence, and Hood could do nothing to soften the blow.

'I know we're heavily outnumbered,' he said. 'Even using the MIPs we can only increase the

44

apparent size of our fleet to three hundred. But we do have some advantages, the most important of which is that the K'Thraa don't know we're coming. And we're going to attack them from where they least expect it – from behind.'

The image of the screen blinked out, to be replaced by a graphic representation of the K'Thraa ships clustered in a oval shape.

'That's the formation they're flying in,' Hood told the crews. 'They're sticking close together for protection, but this means that the ships inside the cluster can't use their energy cannon without the risk of hitting their own ships on the outside. We're not going to make the same mistake.'

A shape like a crescent moon appeared to the left of the oval, its two furthest points curving towards it. The result was to make the crescent look like a gaping mouth about to swallow a plum.

'We're going to warp-jump so that we materialize in space immediately *behind* the K'Thraa fleet,' Hood said. 'We'll be flying in a sickle formation, and we're going to close around the cluster with all our cannon blazing. Given the advantage of surprise, there's no reason why we shouldn't be able to decimate them before they even know we've arrived.'

The screen now showed the crescent closing around the oval and crushing it so that it withered away. Some of the crews began cheering again, and Hood thought, *I only hope it's that easy when we come to the real thing*.

'One question,' said a pilot. 'If we point our ships at Earth, then warp-jump, won't we be facing the wrong way to attack the fleet?'

45

'Good point,' said Hood. 'That's why we're going to be jumping *backwards* through space.'

The pilots looked surprised at first; then they started grinning at the sheer audacity of the tactic. The ships' warp-drives could just as easily carry them backwards as forwards, but it was, nevertheless, a novel idea for attacking an enemy.

'All right,' said Hood, 'any other questions?'

There were none.

'Then let's go!'

The crews began hurrying off to their ships. Hood was glad that no one had asked him the other obvious question: what about all the other K'Thraa starships which were based on Earth? Ro'Sharok was sending only a fraction of his total fleet into space, but once Hood's ships engaged with them near Earth, there was nothing to stop the alien emperor from launching the rest as emergency reinforcements. Their only hope was to destroy the advance guard as quickly as possible, then warp-jump to safety.

Hood left the hall to find Leon and Marianne waiting for him outside. Leon had originally planned to lead the fleet against the K'Thraa in the *Free Earth*. But a few hours ago the flagship had developed a minor fault in its gravity generator which meant that it would not be spaceworthy for several hours.

'Are the crews ready?' Leon asked.

'They're ready,' Hood told him.

'What's morale like?'

'As good as can be expected. They won't let you down.'

'I only wish I was coming with you right now. As

46

soon as the *Free Earth*'s ready, I'll be joining you with as many extra ships as we can muster.'

'Let's just hope that we're still around to greet you,' Hood said grimly. He turned to Marianne. 'Have you managed to get us a crew?'

Hood had not had time to select new gunners for *The White Swan* himself, so he had left the task to Marianne.

'I've got two volunteers who are keen to join us,' she told him.

From a side door two figures stepped into view – councillors Selen and Gorwalden.

'We're ready to fly with you,' Selen said, smiling. 'We'll put ourselves entirely under your command.'

Hood stared at her, then at Gorwalden.

'Are you serious?' he asked.

'Of course we're serious,' Gorwalden said as if offended. 'You practically accused me of wanting to stay here in safety while others do the fighting. Well, I'm ready to show you that I'm not afraid to risk my life for our cause.'

'But you've got no experience of flying in starships.'

'He's been practising in a simulator for the past two days,' Marianne said.

'Gunnery practice,' Gorwalden confirmed. 'And now I'm perfectly capable of handling an energy cannon.'

Hood glanced at Selen, who still had a faint smile on her face. He knew she was a reasonably experienced pilot who had commanded a routine reconnaissance flight around Jupiter only a few weeks ago.

'We won't let you down,' she said simply.

47

There was no time to deliberate over the decision.

'All right,' said Hood, 'let's go!'

Leon wished them good luck, and they headed off, taking an escalator which carried them up to *The White Swan*'s docking bay. There they found Will Redman and Big Mac waiting for them.

'What do you want?' Hood asked sullenly.

'We've come to fly with you,' Will said.

'You told me you were crewing with Leon.'

'We want to fly with the advance fleet,' said Mac. 'So we asked for a transfer.'

'Did you now?'

'We did. If you'll be having us, we'll be at your side.'

'Thanks – but no thanks. I've already got a crew.' Hood swept past them on to the ramp which led up to the main air-lock.

The computer display on the flight-panel showed that the fleet had assembled in the correct crescent formation. They were still in the dense Jovian atmosphere, hovering in sight of the Worldship, and the usual practice was to fly out into space before they made warp-jump. But it would have taken over an hour to rise out of the atmosphere at sub-warp speeds, and time was of the essence. They were going to jump through hyperspace immediately.

'Ten seconds and counting,' Hood said into the radio.

The Worldship hung in the swirling rust-coloured clouds in front of them, a black sphere banded with gold and silver. Hood wondered if he would ever see it again.

Marianne sat beside him, her finger poised on the

star-shaped warp-jump button. She had not spoken to him since they had boarded the ship, and he knew she was furious with him for his treatment of Will and Mac. He had not meant to be so rude, but his pride had got the better of him. Both men were the best gunners in the fleet, and he had rejected them for the uncertain skills of Selen and Gorwalden. The two council members were now installed in the cannon-turrets on both wings of the battlecruiser.

'Three seconds,' said Marianne. 'Two . . . one . . . zero.'

She punched the warp-drive button.

A split-second later, both the Worldship and the restless Jovian atmosphere around it turned transparent, then suddenly blinked out to leave only blackness. An instant after that, the stars winked on, and they were back in normal space.

With the K'Thraa fleet dead ahead of them.

The alien starships were all dull black in colour, with slit-like portholes through which a reddish light gleamed. They were still clustered together in a tight oval, patches of sunlight glowing on their wedge-shaped noses.

The White Swan was flying at the centre of the crescent, and through the main viewport Hood could see that the ships on both edges of the formation had materialized in position. The computer display confirmed that all the ships had made a safe jump through hyperspace. It showed ten times as many ships as there really were, the other pilots having activated their MIP units immediately they jumped into hyperspace. As far as the K'Thraa were concerned, they would only outnumber Hood's fleet by four to three instead of forty to three.

'OK,' Hood shouted into the radio, 'close in and fire when ready!'

The two 'hooks' of the crescent began to draw inwards towards the K'Thraa cluster as they accelerated at sub-warp speed. Marianne punched a button on the flight-panel.

'Anti-matter torpedoes launched,' she said.

Silver cylinders were streaking towards the cluster from all of Hood's ships. Seconds later, they struck home.

The explosions were soundless in the vacuum of space, but fireballs erupted all around the cluster like bright flowers of gold and orange and red.

At least a dozen ships were totally destroyed in the first salvo, and others were mortally damaged. Trailing fire, they veered away from the cluster, thus exposing more to attack.

Hood's ships closed swiftly in, bombarding the cluster from all sides. Both Selen and Gorwalden were poised in their gunnery positions, ready to open fire with their energy cannons on any K'Thraa ships which broke formation and tried to attack or flee. But none did. They maintained their positions even though they were being annihilated.

'It's like shooting fish in a barrel!' Gorwalden said across the intercom. He sounded gleeful and not a little relieved.

'Why are they offering no resistance?' Selen wanted to know. 'None of them are even firing back at us.'

Marianne said, 'We must have hit them just as they were about to warp-jump.'

Hood immediately knew that she was right. The K'Thraa crews were doubtless sealed in the pods so that they wouldn't be killed by hyperspatial concussion on warp-jumping. The humans were immune to this danger by virtue of special pills which protected them.

Hood's fleet closed remorselessly on the rapidly dwindling K'Thraa force. The black starships were being destroyed in great numbers, and the biggest danger to Hood's crews was that of flying debris which could puncture a hull or damage a drive-unit. The bridge of *The White Swan* was filled with flashes of light from explosions, and Hood could hear Gorwalden crying out with glee every time another vessel was destroyed.

Soon it was all over. Not one K'Thraa ship had offered any resistance whatsoever, and the last of the cluster were destroyed by a final salvo of torpedoes from *The White Swan* itself.

Suddenly nothing remained in space where the K'Thraa fleet had been except for fragments of hulls which tumbled outward into the void. An eerie silence descended. None of Hood's crews could believe that they had won so easily.

'We did it,' someone finally murmured across the radio. And then the whole fleet erupted in cheering.

Everyone had anticipated a battle lasting a few hours at least, but they had destroyed the entire fleet in under thirty minutes. The original plan had been for Hood's ships to hold out as long as they could until Leon and the rest of the fleet could reinforce them. Or, if they were being heavily defeated, there was an emergency plan for the ships to warp-jump into the safety of Venus's dense atmosphere, there to lie in wait until they could resume their attack.

'So what do we do now?' Marianne asked.

They were lying ten million kilometres out from Earth – a crescent Earth whose blue seas were tinged with red as a result of the filter in the K'Thraa solar mirror.

'We're going to make another short warp-jump,' Hood said. 'And then we're going to put that solar mirror into reverse.'

The fleet regrouped into an arrowhead formation, Hood informing the other crews of his plan. Marianne manoeuvred a joystick until the crosspiece on a screen was centred near an image of the mirror.

'We're targetted,' she said.

'Then let's go.

She hit the warp-drive button, and space flickered, then reformed around them. Dead ahead was the solar mirror, a huge circular structure built of hexagonal sections which shone red. It looked like a firelit honeycomb.

A button on the flight-panel directly in front of Hood activated the signal which would put the solar mirror into reverse. All the ships in Hood's fleet had been equipped with one, but *The White Swan* was closest to the mirror, and Hood was determined that the honour should fall to him.

With the heel of his hand he hit the button hard. He was staring out at the mirror, but for a second or two nothing happened. Then suddenly the mirror changed colour in the wink of an eye, its fiery red turning to an ice-blue.

'We've done it!' Hood cried.

But his triumph was short-lived, for Marianne was pointing anxiously at one of the scanners.

The scanner showed an image of the crescent

Earth, and at first all Hood registered was the fact that the planet had returned to its normal blue. Then he saw the armada of K'Thraa ships speeding from the night-side of the planet towards them.

7

Hood realized instantly that the second K'Thraa fleet had an overwhelming superiority of numbers. It contained more ships than could be counted, and they were flying in a zig-zag formation so that there was no chance of surrounding them.

And they were closing fast. Ro'Sharok had evidently anticipated an attack on his first fleet, and he had been prepared to sacrifice them so that his enemies would be lured into a trap. Starships needed at least fifteen minutes between warp-jumps to allow the hyperspace drive to recharge, and the K'Thraa fleet would be on them before then.

'Take evasive action!' Hood ordered his crews across the radio. And he himself turned *The White Swan* into a steep dive down towards Earth itself.

His plan was to swoop under the K'Thraa fleet and attack the vulnerable bellies of the vessels. But one of the alien starships immediately broke formation, heading after them.

One of the battlecruiser's scanners had picked up the ship, and Hood stared at the image on the screen in amazement. It was a craft with a long neck and swept-back wings – identical to *The White Swan* itself except that it was painted black.

It was not altogether surprising that Ro'Sharok had built a new flagship to replace *The White Swan* after it had been stolen. But Hood had not expected it to be the mirror-image of his own ship.

'Do you think Ro'Sharok's piloting it?' Marianne asked.

'I doubt it,' Hood said. 'I doubt if he's even on board.' The alien emperor was hugely fat, and Hood suspected that he had never actually seen battle but had merely been the overlord for the aliens' wars.

Hood accelerated *The White Swan* to maximum sub-warp speed. The black starship matched them, staying close on their heels and gradually gaining ground. This was another thing that I should have anticipated, Hood thought – the design has been improved.

Suddenly the black starship opened fire with its energy cannons. Hood was certain that they were out of range, but at that instant the battlecruiser was rocked by explosions.

Marianne checked the monitors for any hint of damage.

'We're OK,' she announced. 'But if we're hit at closer range, the blasts may penetrate our armour. The cannons are more powerful than any we've encountered before.'

'Selen?' Hood said into the intercom. 'Gorwalden? You both all right?'

'I'm fine,' said Selen.

It was a moment before Gorwalden said, 'What are our chances?'

'Stand by with your cannons,' Hood said, 'we're going to do a somersault.'

He pulled hard on the controls, and suddenly the battlecruiser began to turn head over heels and sweep back in the direction from which it had come. The engines were screaming with the strain of the manoeuvre and for a moment the artificial gravity on board the ship went haywire. Had Hood and Marianne not been strapped into their seats, they would have been flung all over the flight-deck.

The manoeuvre was too unexpected for the pilot of the black ship. *The White Swan* was now racing towards it, and Hood yelled to Selen and Gorwalden to open fire.

They did so, and scarlet energy beams flashed from both wings. But their inexperience told against them – both shots missed widely.

Marianne launched a cluster of anti-matter torpedoes, and these sped on target towards their enemy. But at the last second, the K'Thraa pilot executed a flip which caused the torpedoes to flash past both its flanks.

Hood accelerated away, heading inwards towards the Sun. Seconds later, the black ship was on their heels once more.

'If we can hold out for another five minutes,' Marianne said, 'then we can warp-jump.'

Hood nodded grimly. If the black ship followed them through warp-space, its crew would have to enter the protective pods and they would then be as vulnerable as the fleet which had been destroyed.

'I'm targetting us to come out near Venus,' Marianne said, 'just in case we need to take cover in its clouds.'

Hood fed full power into the engines, but gradually the black ship began to gain on them once more. It had not yet launched any anti-matter torpedoes, and Hood found this both strange and worrying. The torpedoes were far more effective weapons for destroying starships than energy cannon fire, and he was sure the ship would be armed with them. Was the K'Thraa pilot simply demonstrating the superiority of his craft before he finally annihilated them?

Selen and Gorwalden's cannons in the wings could only fire forward, and the rear-firing cannon turret on the battlecruiser's broad back was unoccupied. Hood was angry with himself for letting his pride allow him to reject the services of Will and Mac. It was a mistake that might mean the death of them.

The black ship opened fire again, and *The White Swan* was rocked with explosions.

'Energy armour's still holding,' Marianne informed him. 'But I think we're going to have to warp-jump now.'

A digital read-out on the flight-panel indicated that there were still thirty seconds before the warp-drive would be fully recharged. But they didn't have any more time. Hood nodded at Marianne, and she punched the star-button.

The gamble paid off. After giving a frightening lurch, *The White Swan* leapt through hyperspace. As the stars blinked on again, the bridge was bathed in white light – a light reflected from the dense clouds of Venus.

The planet filled most of the viewport, for they had warp-jumped very close to it. Marianne was studying the scanners, and suddenly she said, 'They've followed us.'

The black ship was behind them.

Hood gave a smile. 'We're going to hit them before they can get out of the pods.'

Already he was swinging the battlecruiser around. They began to accelerate towards the black ship.

'Shall I launch the torpedoes?' Marianne asked.

'No,' said Hood, 'let's wait until we're close enough that we can't miss.'

They raced forward, the black ship looming larger in the viewport. But Hood's determination to reach the point-blank range cost them dear. Suddenly, without warning, the black ship opened fire with its energy cannons.

The White Swan was hit head-on, and Hood was smashed against the head-rest of his seat. He blacked out . . .

Struggling up out of unconsciousness, Hood found Marianne wrestling with the battlecruiser's controls. The white clouds of Venus were much closer.

'The blasts have damaged our guidance systems,' she told him. 'We're being pulled down towards Venus.'

Hood's head was pounding, but he took over the controls while Marianne spoke into the intercom:

'Selen? Gorwalden? You all right?'

There was no reply from either.

They were rushing headlong down towards Venus, and within minutes the thick clouds of the planet had swallowed them. There was no time to check the safety of the two council members. Marianne unbolted a section of the flight-panel and took a tool-kit out from under her seat. She had done an intensive course of starship engineering at the Worldship, and she was determined to repair the guidance system. Meanwhile Hood wrestled to keep the battlecruiser in as stable a flight-path as possible.

After about five minutes of flying through dense clouds, *The White Swan* broke through into clear air. Far below they could see the rocky surface of the planet, and there were gleaming stretches of what seemed to be lakes and seas.

'I don't get it,' Hood said. 'The scanners are indicating a surface temperature of thirty degrees celsius, with atmospheric oxygen and no trace of toxic gases. I thought Venus was supposed to be an inferno, with temperatures of hundreds of degrees, sulphuric acid clouds and carbon dioxide everywhere.'

Marianne was too busy to do anything but murmur, 'Must be the Aphrodite Project.'

Hood remembered. The Aphrodite Project had begun fifty years before in the hope of turning Venus into a planet which could be colonized by the human race. Blue-green algae and genetically engineered bacteria had been released into the atmosphere to convert the carbon dioxide into breathable oxygen and lower the temperature. At the time, the scientists involved in the project had estimated that it would be at least a century before the planet became remotely Earth-like. But evidently their algae and bacteria had done the job faster than they had imagined.

Hood decided that he would attempt an emergency landing on one of the seas if Marianne failed to repair the guidance systems. *The White Swan* was designed to float, and there would be less impact on hitting water than land. But as the surface of the planet rushed towards them, Marianne suddenly shouted, 'I think I've got it!'

At that point the malfunction light on the guidance system indicator winked out, and Hood felt the battlecruiser's controls responding fully to him once more.

They were plummeting towards a ridge of jagged mountains, but at the last moment Hood managed to pull the battlecruiser out of its dive so that it flashed narrowly past the peaks. Above them they could see the sun shining fuzzily through the thick upper clouds, and a broad sea to their left gleamed like molten silver.

The pilot of the black starship had evidently assumed that they were mortally damaged and had not pursued them down into Venus's atmosphere. Hood immediately put the battlecruiser into a steep climb. Its scanners showed that no other starship was in the vicinity of Venus, and so the rest of his fleet had to be fighting the K'Thraa armada near Earth. He intended to join them as quickly as possible.

Just then, the whole flight-deck was filled with a klaxon alarm. On the flight-panel the words UNAUTHORIZED ENTRY were flashing, and a computer graphic indicated that someone had entered the warp-drive bay.

Both Hood and Marianne immediately suspected sabotage, since there was no reason for anyone to enter the bay under normal circumstances. Leaving the ship on automatic ascent, they raced down the gangways, their needle-guns at the ready.

When they reached the bay they found Selen standing over the body of Gorwalden. She, too, was holding a needle-gun, and a dart was embedded in Gorwalden's chest.

'What's going on?' Hood asked instantly.

'Gorwalden,' she said. 'He abandoned his turret position, and I came to look for him. I found him here, trying to wreck the tachyon feed channels.'

60

Four pipe-like channels fed faster-than-light particles into the warp-drive chamber. A valve on one of these had been smashed, a wrench lying on the floor near it.

Selen suddenly stumbled forward, and Hood saw the dart which was embedded in a blood-red patch on the upper arm of her tunic. He caught her before she fell, then sat her down on a maintenance platform.

'He tried to shoot me,' she said. 'I had no alternative but to defend myself.'

Gorwalden had a needle-gun in his own hand, his finger still tight around the firing button. Selen's wound was not serious, but the dart would have to be removed and the puncture-hole sterilized.

Marianne was inspecting the damaged valve.

'It's just as well you did stop him,' she said to Selen. 'Another few minutes and he'd have wrecked the warp-drive entirely.'

'Can you repair it?' Hood asked her.

'I think so.' There was a tool-kit on the wall nearby, and she immediately set to work.

Hood led Selen back to the bridge and produced the first-aid kit. Within minutes he had anaesthetized the wound, removed the dart and bound Selen's arm with a sterilizing bandage.

'Why?' Hood wondered aloud. 'I don't understand it. Why should Gorwalden want to sabotage the warp-drive?'

'I don't think he was on our side,' Selen said.

'Well, I know he didn't like me much, but that can't be the reason. Do you think it was cowardice? Perhaps he wanted to stop us from returning to the battle so that it wouldn't have to risk his life again.'

'That wasn't what I meant. I think he was a mole.'

'A mole?'

'No one's yet found out how Ro'Sharok discovered the Worldship's location, but it must have been through someone who betrayed our cause. And I think that someone was Gorwalden.'

Marianne had returned to the flight-deck to pick up a few more tools.

'It makes sense,' she agreed. 'Why else would he want to sabotage *The White Swan*?'

So, Gorwalden was the traitor they had been hoping to uncover. Yet though he had disliked the man, Hood found this surprising. Gorwalden was stubborn, pompous and of questionable courage, but Hood had never doubted his commitment to their cause. But there could be no other reason for his behaviour.

Selen was weak from her wound, but she insisted on remaining beside Hood in the co-pilot's seat. Soon the clouds of Venus dropped away as they emerged into space, and Marianne returned with the news that the valve had been repaired.

'We can make warp-jump when you're ready,' she told Hood.

They had been away from the battle for over an hour, and they would be rejoining a heavily outnumbered fleet. It was ominous that none of Hood's ships had sought sanctuary under Venus's clouds as originally planned. Had they all been destroyed by the K'Thraa armada? And would Hood be better advised to warp-jump back to Jupiter and wait until the rest of the fleet were ready?

No, he could not abandon his other ships, even if they were being massacred. As Marianne replaced Selen in the co-pilot's seat, he turned to her and said, 'Let's get back to the fight.'

8

Emerging out of warp-space, they found themselves in the thick of the battle. Ruby-red tracers of energy-cannon fire streaked across the blackness of space in all directions, and there were starships everywhere – most of them the black vessels of the K'Thraa.

Marianne focused the battlecruiser's scanners on the surrounding ships, and the tactical computer began a rapid count of blue-and-white craft.

The initial results were encouraging. Hood watched the illuminated figures on the computer panel creep towards twenty, suggesting that only a third of the ships had been lost. Then, in a flurry, the numbers flashed past twenty and crept towards thirty.

Had reinforcements arrived from the Worldship? With a sense of despair, Hood realized his mistake as the final total reached forty – the computer was counting the MIP hologram images! And assuming that each craft was generating nine other images like itself, this meant that only four actually remained.

Hood opened a radio channel to the surviving ships while Marianne unleashed a cluster of torpedoes at a K'Thraa vessel. The angular black craft exploded in the viewport as she scored a direct hit, and then Hood heard the anxious voices of his other pilots.

'What's happening?' he asked them. 'Why haven't you warp-jumped to safety?'

Over the jumble of voices, a woman pilot made herself heard: 'We can't. The K'Thraa ships are transmitting some kind of radiation which interferes with the drives. We can't get into hyperspace.'

So the aliens had developed their own secret weapon – and a lethal one. Both Hood and Leon had been relying on the fact that they could gain tactical advantage from frequent leaps through hyperspace. Without that advantage, there was no hope of them overcoming the far more massive K'Thraa fleet. Their own warp-jump to Venus must have been made before the alien armada started transmitting the radiation. Hood had the suspicion that the pilot of *The Black Swan* – as he now thought of it – had wanted to hunt him down personally and destroy him.

There was no sign of the black ship at that moment, though Hood was confident that it had rejoined the armada.

'Fly towards me,' he ordered the surviving pilots, 'and take up defensive formation.'

Hood was proud that his small fleet had lasted as long as an hour when hugely outnumbered by the K'Thraa. All four surviving ships were generating ghost images and using them expertly to confuse the alien fleet. Marianne now activated *The White Swan*'s own MIP unit to give them a little breathing space.

Hood had no real plan since there was no hope of any of them escaping now. But he was determined that they would all die with their weapons blazing. He heard a scream across the radio on one of the channels, followed by an abrupt silence. Beside him, Marianne merely pointed at a scanner, which

64

showed one of the four ships erupting in space so fiercely that Hood knew its main drive units had received a direct hit.

The three surviving ships closed around *The White Swan*, and they formed a tight group, facing outward from one another so that they could give covering fire to their neighbours.

With all four ships generating ghost images, the cluster looked far larger than it actually was. As the K'Thraa armada closed on them, the alien gunners concentrated their fire-power on the outer holo-images. Hood's pilots could cause such images to 'explode' by feeding the appropriate instruction into the MIP unit, and then generate a new image of an intact ship nearby in space. For the K'Thraa, the effect was of destroying one ship, only to have another pop into existence almost immediately.

This would have been enough to confuse and demoralize the alien fleet had it been roughly the same size as their own at the outset of the engagement. But the immense fire-power at the armada's disposal meant that sooner or later they would hit a real ship and destroy all its ghost images with it.

The K'Thraa fleet closed in on all sides, cannon-fire and anti-matter torpedoes flashing through space. Hood felt Marianne's hand close around his wrist, and he met her eyes for what he expected to be the last time.

Suddenly Selen cried, 'Look!'

The councillor was sitting near the viewport, and she was pointing through it. Hood glanced up, and stared in amazement at what he saw.

The K'Thraa ships were going haywire.

Seconds before, the armada had been closing on

them in a tight formation, but now all the ships were veering off course. Even as they watched, some began to collide, while others were flipping head-over-heels or spinning on their axes. Then Hood saw the cause of their disarray.

Leon and the rest of his fleet had materialized in space behind the K'Thraa armada. His star-shaped flagship was leading the attack, a glorious sight as the sunlight flashed on its blue-and-white hull.

The alien armada still outnumbered the ships of the Free Forces of Earth, but the K'Thraa pilots were no longer masters of their craft. It was as if a plague of madness had suddenly afflicted them all so that they had lost control. The blue and white starships of Leon's fleet closed in for the kill.

Hood and his surviving three ships were quick to join the attack, firing off salvoes of torpedoes. Though out of control, the K'Thraa ships were still dangerous since their energy cannons were blazing wildly; and though they were easy targets, there were still hundreds of them. But they were running amok, crashing into one another or veering off into deep space.

Not all the ships were blasted out of existence with torpedoes and cannon fire. Many were boarded by teams of space-suited soldiers who launched themselves with jet-packs from the bellies of Leon's fleet. They employed laser-scythes and limpet mines to cut or blast their way into the K'Thraa starships, using tactics perfected under Hood's command over the past two years. The more ships they could capture intact, the more could be added to their fleet.

After half an hour, *The White Swan* suddenly ran

out of torpedoes. Both Marianne and Selen were eager to man the energy-cannon turrets in the wings so that they could resume the fight, but Hood was taking no chances. He had been trying to contact the *Free Earth* since Leon's fleet had arrived. Both ships carried audio-visual links, and now the screen lit up, showing Leon's bearded face. He was smiling broadly.

'Hood,' he said, 'I'm glad to see you.'

'Not half as glad as I am to see you,' Hood responded with a laugh. 'You arrived just in the nick of time.'

'We came as quickly as we could. How many ships did you lose?'

'All but three, not counting *The White Swan*. But they put up a tremendous fight against overwhelming odds.'

Leon nodded gravely. 'They bought enough time for the rest of us to get here. How d'you think we're doing?'

'Terrific. What's happened to the K'Thraa fleet? They seem to have gone berserk.'

'It's the secret weapon Fitzwalter and AMOS were working on before you left – a K'Thraa destabilizer. We installed it in the *Free Earth* just before we left the Worldship. It transmits radiation which affects the aliens' coordination so that they go into a frenzy and can't control their ships. Makes them sitting targets for us. Pity we can't beam it all over the planet to send the ground forces mad, but AMOS tells me it won't work in air.'

'Is my father with you?' Marianne asked.

Leon shook his head. 'He's still at the Worldship,

67

working on yet another surprise for the K'Thraa. I don't know what we'd have done without him.'

Leon suddenly glanced aside, as if one of his crew had spoken to him.

'We'd better get on with this battle,' he said to Hood. 'There'll be time for talking later.'

'I need some gunners,' Hood told him. 'We're out of torpedoes, Selen's injured and Gorwalden is dead –'

'Dead? What happened to him?'

'Selen caught him trying to sabotage our warp-drive. It looks as if he was the K'Thraa spy who revealed the Worldship's location to Ro'Sharok.'

Leon looked solemn for a moment. 'Is Selen all right?'

'She's got a wounded arm – nothing serious. But we need gunners for our cannon turrets. Can you spare anyone?'

Leon eyed him. 'Did you have any particular persons in mind?'

'Yes,' Hood said without hesitation. 'Will Redman and Big Mac. I've treated them badly of late, but there's no better gunners in the whole fleet. If they want to come, I'd welcome them with open arms.'

There was a hint of a grin under Leon's profuse beard.

'I'll see what I can do,' he said.

Hood kept *The White Swan* out of the heat of the battle for the next ten minutes. He flew towards the *Free Earth*, narrowing the gap between the two ships as much as possible. Presently Marianne said, 'Here they come.'

One of the radar screens showed four small blobs

emerging from the larger image of the flagship. A few minutes later, a scanner picked them up. There were three figures in spacesuits, accompanied by a large silver egg. The last had no jet-pack but was being propelled through space on a short tail of white fire which spurted from its blunt end.

Marianne opened an air-lock in the body of the battlecruiser to receive them.

'I'll take over the controls,' she said to Hood. 'You can go and meet them. I'm sure you'll want to have a few minutes alone.'

Hood did not grasp her meaning. 'Alone? Why?'

'To apologize, Hood.' She sounded like a teacher addressing a dimwitted child. 'I think they deserve it, don't you?'

'We don't even know it's going to be Will and Mac.'

'But if it is?'

Hood was fully aware of how stubborn and inconsiderate he had been towards his two lieutenants.

'Well?' Marianne prompted.

'I'll apologize,' he said.

When he arrived at the air-lock, an indicator light told him that his new gunners were aboard. He swung open the hatch, and there stood Big Mac, Will Redman and Mitch Miller. They had just removed their spacesuit helmets. Beside them was the silver egg.

'I think we'll leave him in there,' Will Redman was saying to Mac. 'I like the look of him better.'

'I am perfectly capable of hearing you,' said the muffled voice of AMOS from inside the egg. 'Your feeble attempts at humour are not the slightest bit amusing. Please release me immediately.'

'Please release me,' Will began singing in a cracked voice, 'let me go. I'm stuck in here and feeling sore . . .'

Will was resting a hand on the metal egg encasing AMOS. Suddenly he yelped and jerked his hand away.

'A mild electric shock,' AMOS informed him. 'Next time I shall use a stronger current.'

Mac, grinning through his beard, pressed a button at the top of the egg which caused it to unfold in quarter segments like the rind of a fruit. The egg was designed to protect AMOS's micro-circuitry from damage as he travelled through space. A rocket built into its base provided the propulsion, and AMOS could control his direction from inside.

AMOS now glided out of the unfolded egg while Will glowered at him, still nursing his hand.

'We should have left you behind with Leon,' Will grumbled, 'you overgrown excuse for a ball bearing.'

'Your persistent abuse of me,' retorted AMOS, 'suggests that secretly you admire me but are afraid to admit it to yourself.'

'Admire?! You've got to be kidding. If I ever ended up admiring you, then I'd know I've really lost my marbles.'

'That is a contradiction in terms. If you lost your marbles, as you so colourfully put it, then you would not be aware of the fact. Insanity – '

'You're so literal-minded. You might be intelligent, but you've got no imagination.'

Big Mac and Mitch were listening to the argument with long-suffering smiles. Will and AMOS were always at loggerheads. They had not noticed Hood, so he cleared his throat to gain their attention.

70

'I'm sorry to break up this fascinating conversation,' he said drily, 'but we've got work to do.'

They immediately emerged from the air-lock, Will, Mac and Mitch stripping off their spacesuits. Will had stuffed his three-cornered hat into one of the inner pockets of his suit, and he now unfolded it and put it on.

'Thanks for coming,' Hood said to them, 'I appreciate it.'

'Once we heard you wanted us,' said Mac, 'then nothing would have kept us away. Isn't it our ship as much as yours?'

'It is indeed,' Hood replied. 'I shouldn't have left you behind in the first place. I owe you an apology.'

'Think nothing of it,' said Mac.

'No, Mac, I've been pig-headed and I've taken you for granted. But that's not going to happen again. From now on, we work together as equals.'

Suddenly they heard Marianne's voice across the intercom: 'Hood, I think you'd better get back here immediately.'

All five of them hurried down the gangways to the bridge.

Beyond the viewport, space was filled with a scattering of K'Thraa ships which were being pursued and destroyed by Leon's fleet. But Marianne was pointing to a scanner on the flight-panel. It showed *The Black Swan*.

'It's heading for the *Free Earth*,' Marianne told him.

'It's under control?' he said, disbelieving.

She nodded. 'It seems to unaffected by the radiation which the *Free Earth* is transmitting. And if it knocks out the flagship, then the rest of the K'Thraa

71

armada are going to be back in action again. And there's still a lot of their ships left.'

As briefly as possible, Hood told the others about their earlier encounters with *The Black Swan* and how it had almost destroyed them. At this point Selen, who had been sitting silently near Marianne, suddenly slumped off her seat in a faint.

Marianne rushed to her side. The arm of the councillor's tunic was red from elbow to wrist.

'It must be loss of blood,' Hood said. 'AMOS, you're going to have to attend to her.'

'I assumed you wanted me to man the tail-firing cannon.' AMOS said.

'And so I did. But Selen needs treatment, and you're the best equipped to give her it.'

'I'll take the tail-firing cannon,' Mitch said.

He looked eager to do his part, but he was just a teenager, with no experience of space-battles. Hood glanced at Mac.

'He'll not let you down,' Mac told him. 'Hours he's spent practising on the cannon simulators at the Worldship. He has a keen eye and a steady hand.'

There was no time for dithering. 'All right,' Hood said, 'to your positions!'

9

'It's closing fast,' Marianne said to Hood.

He glanced down at the radar scanner. The blip which indicated the black ship was moving rapidly towards the *Free Earth*. Since dispatching Mac and the others to *The White Swan*, Leon's flagship had moved to another sector of space in pursuit of a K'Thraa vessel. It now lay several millions of kilometres distant from Hood's battlecruiser.

'We're too far away,' he said to Marianne. 'We're not going to be able to intercept it in time.'

'We will if we can warp-jump,' she replied.

She was already targetting the battlecruiser to emerge in space near its black counterpart.

'But we can't . . .' Hood began, then stopped, seeing Marianne's reasoning. The K'Thraa armada had been broadcasting signals designed to prevent the warp-drives from operating. But now that the armada had been driven haywire by the professor and AMOS's device, then perhaps the drives would function again.

Crossing her fingers. Marianne said, 'Let's give it a try.'

She punched the button.

And the battlecruiser jumped.

Suddenly both the *Free Earth* and *The Black Swan* hung in space in front of them. Leon's flagship had just destroyed another K'Thraa vessel, and it had evidently not noticed the black ship's approach. A cluster of anti-matter torpedoes was already heading it.

'We're too late,' Hood said with dismay.

But he had not counted on Mac and Will's experience. Rather than aiming at *The Black Swan*, they directed their cannon-fire at the torpedoes themselves, exploding them in space before they could hit Leon's vessel.

The flagship immediately executed a tight turn and began closing on the black ship in the opposite direction from the *The White Swan*.

'We've got him now,' Hood heard Will Redman say from his turret in the wing. He sounded gleeful.

Suddenly the black ship vanished.

'It's warp-jumped,' Marianne said.

But how? Hood wondered. How could the K'Thraa on board be immune to the disruptor device when the rest of the armada was not? The only answer he could think of was that the ship had special shielding to protect it from the radiation.

Once again there was no time to dwell on the matter, for more K'Thraa ships were pouring up into space from Earth. In a last desperate onslaught, Ro'Sharok was apparently launching all his available craft into space. Only a few were starships, most being smaller craft such as the arrowhead-shaped interceptors and suicide pods which were shaped like grenades.

Once again, though, the disruptor device was the saving of Leon's fleet. As soon as the K'Thraa craft reached space, they immediately went out of control. Hood and the rest of his crew were kept busy for the next hour or so destroying as many as possible. The main danger was of accidental collision with a suicide pod, which was packed with explosives. On their previous mission to Earth Hood and the others had been locked into such a pod on collision course for the Moon. His troops still talked about their last-minute escape with amazement and pride.

They managed to avoid all the pods, blasting them at a safe distance. Hood kept an eye out for *The Black Swan*, but the pilot of the craft was evidently playing hide-and-seek among the rapidly dwindling armada. But Hood was confident that it would appear again.

Another hour passed as *The White Swan* chased down and destroyed any K'Thraa ships they could find. The rest of Leon's fleet were doing the same, all of space within millions of kilometres of Earth their battlefield. By now the fleet had spread out so much in pursuing the out-of-control alien vessels that each ship was effectively alone in space, in touch with others only via radio and radar. It was at this point that Leon ordered a general regrouping.

'Abandon pursuit of any remaining ships,' he told his pilots, 'and return to Earth-vicinity immediately.'

Marianne was quick to point out the reason for this order. On the radar screen which was focused on Earth were several blips that were far larger than any they had seen before.

'I think Ro'Sharok has launched his mother-ships,' she said.

Using their warp-jumps, Leon's fleet swiftly reassembled near Earth. The solar mirror still hung in space, but Earth was now its normal blue once more. And framed by the planet were a dozen enormous craft with swollen bodies and leg-like

75

appendages sticking out from both their sides. They looked like huge, grotesque black spiders.

The mother-ships were each as large as the Worldship, and they had carried the K'Thraa population to Earth from their home planet after the invasion.

'I've a notion it's Ro'Sharok's last gamble,' Mac said across the intercom. 'He's throwing the only ships he has left against us.'

'I think you're right, Mac,' said Hood. 'Those mother-ships are transporters, not battle craft.'

'Attack at will,' came Leon's order.

The White Swan was ahead of the rest of the fleet, and Hood accelerated forward towards the nearest mother-ship. Mac and Will opened fire with their energy cannons, but the scarlet beams bounced harmlessly off the the golden glows which had suddenly flashed on around all the spider-craft.

'They've got giant-sized force-shields,' Marianne said. 'Our cannons are going to be useless against them,'

Hood veered rapidly away as the mother-ship opened fire on the battlecruiser.

'Force-shields won't stop torpedoes,' Will remarked from his turret.

And he was quickly proved right. Two starships following up Hood's attack launched clusters of torpedoes, several of which hit home. Explosions blossomed on the curving hull of the mother-ship, leaving gaping holes in it.

The rest of Leon's fleet closed in. It would take several salvoes of torpedoes to destroy each of the massive craft, but their destruction was inevitable.

They did not have the speed or manoeuvrability to escape their attackers.

'Looks like we'll have to sit this one out,' Hood remarked.

Without torpedoes, *The White Swan* was temporarily neutralized.

'I think we'd better keep moving,' came Mitch's voice from the rear of the ship. 'We've got someone on our tail.'

So intent had they been on attacking the motherships that they had not noticed a vessel creeping up behind them.

It was *The Black Swan*.

This time the pilot of the ship was taking no chances. He had already launched a salvo of antimatter torpedoes.

Hood took evasive action, weaving and darting through space. The torpedoes flashed harmlessly by, but *The Black Swan* remained on the battlecruiser's tail, its pilot matching every manoeuvre of Hood's.

In the rear cannon turret, Mitch had opened fire, but it was difficult for him to take proper aim with the rapid changes in speed and direction which both ships were making. *The Black Swan*'s hull was composed of the same energy-cannon resistant armour as their own ship, but this did not mean that it was invulnerable. 'Aim for the viewport,' Hood told Mitch through the intercom. Tests had shown that *The White Swan* was vulnerable in its bridge section, and Hood was hoping that the same would apply to the black ship.

'I can't even get a bead on it at the moment!' came Mitch's reply.

Hood decided to take a risk. He deliberately

straightened the battlecruiser's trajectory and kept it steady on course, hoping that Mitch would have sufficient time to aim and fire. Marianne switched on the screen to Mitch's turret which showed the aiming crosspiece of his cannon. He had the black ship in his sights, but the crosspiece wavered and flickered around the viewport.

The black ship launched a cloud of silvery spheres which Hood recognized as disruptor mines. A second later, Mitch's crosspiece steadied on the viewport. He fired.

Red tracers flashed across space towards the black ship, and the viewport exploded in a hail of fragments.

Already Hood was taking evasive action against the mines, which were designed to interfere with the molecular bonding between atoms, causing a starship's structure to fall apart. But one of the silver spheres clipped the tip of the starboard wing, which promptly disintegrated.

The damage was minor, only a small section of the wing having been lost. Mac, in the starboard wing cannon turret, was unharmed. But *The White Swan* had lost some of its aerodynamic stability, making it difficult to control.

'I don't believe it,' came the voice of Mitch from his turret. The screen showed the reason for his astonishment. *The Black Swan* was flying down towards Earth in a controlled glide.

The ship's viewport had been blasted away to leave a gaping hole, but there was no doubt that the ship was still being piloted.

'The controls must still be intact,' Marianne said.

'That may be,' Hood replied, 'but it begs the question. The viewport's gone, and all the air in the bridge must have been sucked out into space. *So how can the pilot still be alive?*'

10

'It's heading for Britain,' Marianne remarked.

Hood nodded, concentrating on keeping the black ship in his sights. They had been pursuing it down through the Earth's atmosphere for the past hour, Hood only just managing to keep *The White Swan* on a steady flight-path. Because of the damage to the battlecruiser, he had been forced to keep his distance from the black ship in case it opened fire with its cannon again. Though crippled, it was still a dangerous enemy.

But Hood was determined on a final confrontation. He wasn't going to let it escape now; he wanted to find out just who could be piloting it.

AMOS had returned from the sick-bay after attending to Selen, who was now sleeping. Hood turned to him.

'Do you think the crew could be robots like you?' he asked.

'Unlikely,' AMOS responded. 'We have no evidence that the K'Thraa ever built robots of any sort. In many respects they are more scientifically advanced than us, but not in all.'

'But they can't be ordinary aliens.'

'That is quite true. I have to say that for once I am completely mystified.'

'We're only a few minutes from landfall, Hood,' Marianne remarked. 'What are you going to do?'

'Wait,' he replied. 'Wait, and bide our time. See what it does first.'

Most of Britain was still under darkness, only the easterly edges of England being in sunlight. The land was white. Having descended through the cloud layer, Hood and the others discovered that it was snowing heavily.

The black ship was flying westwards towards the night-line, dropping swiftly but still under control towards the ground. Marianne was studying the radar scanners which showed both *The Black Swan* and the landscape below.

'We're over Essex,' she announced. 'And heading towards London.'

'Jonas,' said Hood. 'He has his palace in London. Do you think it could be him?'

Jonas was an old enemy. Once the Regional Governor of Britain, he had betrayed his people to the K'Thraa during the invasion. As a reward for his treachery, Ro'Sharok allowed him to continue as puppet governor of Britain. From the grim citadel of New Buckingham Palace, he supervised the teams of human slaves who worked on K'Thraa plantations.

'Jonas is only human,' Marianne said. 'If he was flying the ship, he wouldn't have survived when the viewport was blasted away.'

'I agree,' said AMOS. 'There's also no evidence that he has any experience of flying starships. And he's not a man to risk himself in battle if he can possibly avoid it.'

The black ship was slowing rapidly now as it flew over the snow-covered ground. The K'Thraa had planted fast-growing fern-trees over much of Britain to provide themselves with food, but these had rapidly withered under the sudden onslaught of winter. Only their drooping skeletons remained.

They followed the black ship across the night-line into darkness. Somewhere below them lay what was left of London. Most of its buildings had been demolished by the K'Thraa and replaced by plantations. Large cities throughout the world had suffered a similar fate. It was as if the K'Thraa had deliberately obliterated them because they symbolized so many aspects of human achievement.

Marianne, intent on the radar screen, suddenly said, 'It's touched down.'

She punched a keyboard below the screen, and the computer printed out the precise landing point.

'It's a few miles north of Jonas's palace.'

'Landing strip?' asked Hood.

'No sign of one. It must have been an emergency landing.'

'What's the terrain like?'

'Low hills, no vegetation. What used to be Hampstead Heath.'

'It's a sitting target,' said Will from his turret in the wing. 'Shame we haven't got any torpedoes.'

'We aren't going to destroy it,' Hood told him. 'Not yet, at least. I'm going to land nearby. Then we're going to find out what's inside it.'

The landing was tricky with a damaged wing and in adverse weather conditions, but Hood was more careful than he had ever been. The battlecruiser was designed for vertical take-off and landing on any kind of ground that was reasonably firm and level. Hood selected a flat valley between two low hills, cutting the forward thrust to zero and activating the vertical boosters. Then he gradually reduced the boosters' power so that the battlecruiser gently lowered itself to the ground.

They landed with a firm thud, and Hood cut the engines. By now, Will, Mac and Mitch had joined the rest of them in the bridge.

'Well,' Marianne remarked, 'we're back on good old Mother Earth again.'

'Yes,' said Hood. 'Let's make sure that this time we're here to stay!'

Snow was falling thickly as they climbed to the brow of the hill. The sky overhead was black, but the first hints of dawn were visible to the east.

They had left Mitch behind to guard the battlecruiser while they were away. It was unlikely that any K'Thraa troops would come upon the ship in darkness, and he would be safe as long as he kept the hatches closed.

Hood and the others wore white snowsuits which allowed greater freedom of movement than spacesuits. Though it was dark, the carpet of snow provided some visibility. Hood, staring down into the valley beyond the hill, raised a gloved hand and pointed.

'There it is.'

The black ship lay in a broad oval of grass, the snow around it having been melted by the heat of its boosters. It was just possible to see the jagged hole of the shattered viewport through the snow-thick air. The bridge inside was in darkness.

Armed with needle-guns and sonic grenades, Hood and the others descended the hill towards the ship. No one spoke as they approached it with great caution.

The hatches were all sealed, and there was no evidence of any footprints in the vicinity.

'They must be still aboard,' Hood whispered to the others. His breath was like mist in the chill air.

Having completed a circuit of the craft, they paused at its long neck. There was a hatch there which would give them speedy access to the bridge.

'All right,' Hood said. 'We're going in.'

Will Redman produced a handgrip with a button at one end. He pressed the button, and an arc of brilliant white light flared from the end of the handgrip. This was a laser-scythe whose blade could cut through the toughest metal.

With a single stroke, Will sheared away the external lock on the hatch. Then Big Mac stepped forward and swung the heavy door open.

The five of them entered the air-lock, their needle-guns at the ready. The inner hatch could be opened at the press of a button, but Will kept the laser-scythe switched on since it provided light.

Cautiously Big Mac swung open the hatch. Beyond was the dark gangway which led towards the bridge. They could see no sign of movement.

'Switch it off,' Hood said to Will.

Will deactivated the scythe, and they were plunged into darkness again. The scythe would have pinpointed them as easy targets.

'OK,' Hood whispered, 'let's go.'

'We'd be wise to wait a little while,' Mac said, 'till our eyes adjust to the gloom.'

'Good thinking,' said Hood.

They crouched in the hatchway, their pistols

pointed in all directions. After half a minute or so, they were able to pick out general shapes in the darkness.

Hood now moved forward down the gangway, AMOS hovering silently beside him, with Marianne, Mac and Will bringing up the rear. The black ship was utterly silent, and Hood felt like an explorer of a haunted house, not knowing what danger might suddenly confront them.

The main gangway which led to the bridge was intersected at intervals by other corridors. They moved particularly stealthily past these, expecting an attack at any moment. But still none came. Still the ship was silent; still nothing moved.

Finally they approached the doorway to the bridge. Like that aboard *The White Swan*, the door was of the type which opened like a bud unfurling when anyone approached it.

Hood and AMOS edged forward. AMOS carried no needle-gun, but a nozzle in his chest could pour out a black anti-riot tar which engulfed attackers and rapidly solidified, trapping them.

The door blossomed open with a gentle WHOOSH! of air. Hood and AMOS paused on the threshold of the bridge.

All was darkness inside, and Hood could see and hear nothing. But AMOS had keener perceptions, and in a whisper he said: 'They're here.'

For some reason, Hood felt his mouth go dry. He took a step backwards, then stopped. To AMOS he whispered, 'Switch on your chest-beam. Low power, narrow focus.'

A cone of dull creamish light issued from one of the panels in AMOS's chest. It illuminated the gaping hole in the viewport. Then suddenly Hood saw two shadowy figures standing nearby.

AMOS angled the beam so that it fell directly on them. Hood gasped when he saw their faces.

'Adair!' he said. 'Isabelle!'

Adair and Isabelle had joined his army before his first escape from Earth. They had been shot down at Heathrow Spaceport during the hijack of *The White Swan*.

'You're dead,' Hood said disbelievingly. 'The K'Thraa killed you.'

Neither Adair nor Isabelle replied. Hood now saw that their eyes were rolled up in their sockets. They were zombies.

AMOS turned the beam back towards the flight-deck. Two more figures were in the pilots' seats.

'No!' Hood said, his voice fracturing into a sob. 'No!'

It was his mother and father.

A screen lit up on the flight-panel, and at the same time the emergency lights came on.

The alien emperor, Archmaster Ro'Sharok, stared out at them.

Ro'Sharok was grossly fat, and his head was a bluish-grey mound on top of his rounded shoulders. His lips were frog-like, his nose just two flat slits, his eyes swollen and white with black slashes at their centres. Milky lids flashed across them.

'Hood,' the Archmaster said, the word coming out in a hiss. 'This is a recorded message which was activated by the sound of your voice. It is possible that your skill at piloting will prove too much even for this special crew and ship which we sent against you. If it does not, then you will never hear this message.'

Ro'Sharok paused, shifting heavily in his stone-like seat. His whole face wobbled as he did so.

'Still,' he went on, 'any victory will be a hollow one. I am sure you will recognize the crew I sent against you. They were specially picked for the task.' This time there was something like a leer on his amphibian face. He had obviously anticipated the horror that his creations would cause to Hood and the others.

'Of course,' he continued, 'they are not alive in the accepted sense of the word. Adair and Isabelle were on the brink of death, but our drugs froze them on the point of oblivion. It was the same with your parents. They did not die when you crashed the starship into my palace – we lied to you about that. We had them hidden elsewhere. But we *did* destroy them soon afterwards – yet not so absolutely that we couldn't make them into our own creatures, just like Adair and Isabelle.'

Ro'Sharok drew in a blubbery breath. 'Our scientists worked wonders with them, don't you think? They reanimated and reprogrammed them, turning your parents into excellent starship pilots and your two friends into expert energy-cannon gunners. They are all in terrible agony, of course, poised on the brink of death and yearning for release. You may do as you wish with them. They have failed in their mission and are of no further use to us.'

Hood let out a howl of anguish and rage before firing a cluster of darts at the screen, which promptly shattered. It was a futile gesture, he knew, since the Archmaster was far away and must have recorded the message days or weeks before. But he had to strike out at something.

Marianne, Mac and Will had edged into the bridge behind Hood and AMOS, their needle-guns trained on the crew of *The Black Swan* – a crew that had been able to survive even when exposed to the vacuum of space because they were not truly alive.

But they no longer presented any threat. Like puppets held on invisible strings, they had no initiative of their own. Hood's mother and father were slumped in their seats, while the arms of Adair and Isabelle hung limply from their shoulders. But it was their faces which were the most heartbreaking of all. On them was a look of dull agony, as if their inner torment was frozen under the masks of their reprogramming. Like machines or performing animals, they had been trained for a particular task – to fly a starship and track Hood down. But beyond this, they were helpless.

Hood walked slowly over to his parents. Their eyes were rolled upwards so that only the whites could be seen. But even so it seemed as if they were staring at him.

'Mother?' he said in an unsteady voice. 'Father?'

They did not move or react.

Hood could not bear the agony he saw in their faces. He raised his needle-gun and pointed it at them. But he could not bring himself to fire.

Suddenly Will and Mac were standing beside him.

'Leave it to us,' Will said in the gentlest of voices.

'You go outside,' Mac added. 'We'll do what's necessary.'

Both men looked grim. Hood nodded, too numb to argue.

He let Marianne lead him down the gangway and out through the hatch into the snow-thick air. A grey dawn was seeping across the sky, and the wind had risen, driving the snow into drifts like the breakers of a white ocean. Marianne kept a firm hand on Hood's arm, leading him around to the front of the ship.

'Are you all right?' she asked.

Hood nodded, though in fact he was not sure how he was feeling.

'At least you know you weren't responsible for their deaths.'

'Oh, but I am. I could go back in there now and stop the executions.'

'They're mercy killings, Hood. You know that.'

Hood did not reply. He stared up at the bridge. The lights had been switched off again, and all was in darkness. Marianne was right, of course. Nothing could be done to save them. As zombies they were in agony – an agony which could only be relieved by a merciful death.

Suddenly a brilliant white light flashed in the bridge, and there was a terrible piercing scream. In the next few seconds it was repeated three times. Hood had no doubt what was happening: the laser-scythe was being used to put the crew of *The Black Swan* out of their misery as swiftly as possible.

A few minutes later, AMOS, Will and Mac emerged from the ship.

'It's done,' Mac said. 'They're in peace.'

Hood nodded. He did not ask which of them had performed the executions. This was something he never wanted to know.

They began to trudge back through the snow

towards *The White Swan*. In the east the sun was now visible as a golden patch of light behind the clouds. But the wind still drove snow into their faces, and Hood could feel a wetness on his cheeks. Then he tasted salt at the corner of his mouth and realized that the wetness was his own tears.

11

The White Swan sat on a patch of grass that had lost its oval shape as the snow invaded it once more. Hood and the others approached the hatchway nearest the bridge, AMOS opening a communications channel to Mitch on board.

'We are back,' AMOS said. 'Is all well?'

'All's well,' came the reply.

Mitch opened the hatchway automatically from inside. They clambered on board, relieved to be out of the cold.

Hood was still in a state of shock. Ever since the K'Thraa invasion he had had to be strong and brave, an example to all the soldiers in his army. But the stress had told, draining him both physically and mentally. He was not sure he could bounce back from the renewed grief of losing his parents.

Marianne led him forward into the bridge, the doorway blossoming open in front of them. The others followed.

Mitch was standing in front of the pilot's seat, but there was a strange expression on his face. Then Hood saw that behind him, crouching on the seat, was Selen.

She was holding a needle-gun to Mitch's back.

'Stay where you are,' she ordered them. 'Do anything silly and I shoot the boy.'

Big Mac instinctively took a step forward, but Will Redman held him back with a hand on his arm.

'Well, well,' said another voice. 'We meet yet again.'

Out of the shadows behind a bank of instruments, stepped Jonas.

Tall and thin, with a gaunt face and dark hair, Jonas was dressed in his favourite robes of indigo and crimson. Accompanying him were over a dozen K'Thraa stormtroopers, their stub-guns raised. They had been hiding all around the bridge, and now they completely encircled Hood and the others.

The K'Thraa wore mustard-coloured tunics which would have been woefully inadequate to protect them from the chill weather outside; but it was warm inside the ship. They all carried stub-guns which were levelled on Hood and the others. Their skins were slate-grey and did not have the bluish tinge of the ruling caste. These were the warrior aliens, specially bred to be ruthless fighting machines.

One of the K'Thraa now stepped forward and smashed the butt of his stub-gun into AMOS's chest, destroying the nozzle from which AMOS produced his anti-riot tar. Jonas had seen how effective it was as a weapon on previous occasions. He was clearly taking no chances.

'So you were the traitor,' Marianne said to Selen.

Selen smiled, her teeth showing white. 'That fool Gorwalden discovered me as I was about to disable your warp-drive. I had no alternative but to kill him. I think he must have suspected me of not being entirely loyal to your glorious cause. Perhaps that's why he insisted on joining me aboard this ship even though he was a coward.'

'Better a coward than a traitor,' Will Redman said bitterly.

92

'But why?' Marianne wanted to know. 'Why betray your own race?'

'For love,' Jonas said. 'And power.'

Selen was quick to elaborate: 'Before the invasion, Jonas and I were to be married, but I was out in space aboard the Worldship when the K'Thraa launched their attack. I had no choice but to become one of the rebels, bravely battling for the freedom of Earth. Then when I learned that Jonas was not only alive but thriving under the K'Thraa, I determined to take my rightful place beside him.'

Selen had always had a ready smile, and now it seemed positively sinister.

'There was no opportunity to contact him,' she went on, 'until I commanded a reconnaissance ship a few weeks ago. Once we were out of Jupiter's atmosphere, I secretly radioed Earth and arranged a bargain with the K'Thraa. In exchange for revealing the Worldship's location, they promised me that I could join Jonas once all the rebels had been destroyed and share in all his privileges.'

Selen looked positively proud of her treachery, and Will could not restrain his disgust: 'You'd betray every human being in the Solar System just for a slice of power? In my eyes, that makes you lower than a worm's belly.'

Selen was unruffled. 'Sometimes we have to pay a high price for what we want.'

'I pressume,' said AMOS, 'that you joined the crew of *The White Swan* to keep an eye on Hood.'

'Exactly. There was no opportunity to warn Earth that Hood's fleet was being launched. But I was confident that if I bided my time I'd find a way of neutralizing you.'

'She overpowered me,' Mitch said. 'while you were away. I thought she was sleeping in the sick-bay, but she got a needle-gun from one of the spacesuits and crept up on me when I wasn't looking. I didn't have a chance. Then she radioed the palace and contacted Jonas. He came straightaway, and she let him into the ship. I couldn't do anything to stop her.'

Mitch looked crestfallen, as if he had let them all down. But Big Mac was quick to comfort him: 'You weren't to know she was a snake in the grass.'

'Console yourselves while you can,' said Jonas, grinning unpleasantly. 'You're in our hands now, and this time we're not going to let you go.'

Marianne was defiant: 'You're fighting a losing battle, Jonas. Ro'Sharok's fleet has already been destroyed, and Leon will be landing ground forces all over the globe within the next few hours. This time we've got the upper hand.'

Jonas put a pointed fingernail under her chin, forcing her head up. 'Your confidence is touching, but misplaced. Ro'Sharok has assured me that there is no possibility of your invasion being successful. If necessary he will unleash his ultimate weapon which will destroy you all.'

Jonas was digging his fingernail into Marianne's chin so that her face was screwed up with pain. He was staring at Hood as he did so, obviously hoping to provoke a reaction from him. Hood had been silent up to now, and still he did not speak or do anything.

'What's the matter with our great hero?' Jonas asked Marianne. 'Isn't he going to try to protect you?'

'Leave her alone,' Hood said dully. But his grief had turned to despair at their capture, and there was no real force behind his words.

Not that there would have been any use in attempting to fight back. The K'Thraa had stub-guns trained on all of them, and they looked ready to fire at the slightest provocation. The fish-like smell of the aliens was strong in the air. In failing to notice it as they entered the bridge, they had walked into a trap.

Jonas was scrutinizing Hood, and a slow smile formed on his boney face. On his right cheek was as long scar, the result of a knife wound which Adair had inflicted on him during the hijack of *The White Swan*. The scar moved like a rippling snake when he smiled.

'I think your leader has lost his nerve,' he remarked to Marianne and the others. Then he turned to the K'Thraa and said, 'Take them away!'

Jonas's transporter was sitting on the other side of the hill from where *The White Swan* had landed. Hood and the others were bundled into the hold under heavy guard. Before they had left the battle-cruiser, Jonas had AMOS sealed inside the silver egg to ensure that the robot would cause him no trouble. AMOS had succeeded in surprising him in the past, but this time Jonas wasn't going to give him the opportunity.

The transporter took them straight to New Buckingham Palace. The palace had been built fifty years before to replace its predecessor which had been destroyed during the Third World War. It was a grim, daunting structure of concrete blocks and slitted windows which made it look like a military fortress. No other building stood for miles around, just acres of white carpeted fields and lines of withering fern-trees surrounded the palace.

The K'Thraa stormtroopers moved sluggishly in the

snow-filled morning as they herded Hood and the others from the transporter to the palace. They obviously hated the cold, but there were too many of them for the humans to risk an escape attempt. New walls surrounded the grounds of the palace – broad, flat-topped concrete walls with cannon turrets at intervals along them. For all his contempt towards the Free Forces of Earth, Jonas had obviously taken their threat seriously in constructing the defensive walls.

Hood and his friends were bundled into the palace, where a blue-skinned K'Thraa in a white and gold tunic stood waiting.

'This is the Highmaster Hi'Veshezz,' Jonas announced. 'He's one of Ro'Sharok's many nephews. He was transferred here a few weeks ago at his own request from the Archmaster's palace.'

'I wished to ensure that the plantations here were being properly worked,' Hi'Veshezz said haughtily. 'Slave workers must be treated like cattle if the best is to be got out of them.'

Like all other Highmasters – it was a title equivalent to 'prince' – Hi'Veshezz wore a translator at his neck. He was younger than any other K'Thraa aristocrat that Hood had seen before – perhaps the same age as Hood himself. But there was no mistaking the familiar arrogance and hatred in his rasping voice.

'You won't be picking any crops now,' Will Redman said. 'All you'll be picking soon is needle-gun darts out of your backside.'

'You are scum,' Hi'Veshezz replied coldly. 'The sooner you are exterminated, the better.'

Jonas and Selen stood together, Jonas stroking Selen's silver hair.

'Enjoy yourselves while you can,' Will said to them. 'Your time's running out. Whatever happens to us, Earth's going to be liberated and your days are numbered.'

'That remains to be seen,' Jonas replied. 'You have no future, whatever happens. This time we are going to make sure that you do not escape.'

They were bundled through the concrete corridors of the palace, past rooms with slitted windows where K'Thraa with greenish-grey skins were at work. Once, all three K'Thraa races had been equal, but after a war, a breeding programme was begun which segregated them into castes. The green K'Thraa were the slave caste, bred for instant obedience to grey-skinned soldiers and the blue-skinned aristocrats.

The green K'Thraa were operating machines which stitched together padded suits evidently meant for alien stormtroopers fighting in the snow. It was added evidence that Jonas and Hi'Veshezz were expecting an attack on the palace.

The K'Thraa soldiers prodded and pushed the humans down a long flight of stairs to the cellar. On a previous mission to Earth they had been locked in one of the grubby cells there, and this time it was no different except that the cell was already occupied. Sitting on the dirty, straw-littered floor was a blue-skinned female K'Thraa.

'Sha'Rani!' said Marianne on catching sight of her.

'So,' said Jonas, 'you know her name. We suspected she might be a traitor, and now we know there has been contact between you. Ro'Sharok will be most interested.'

All of them except AMOS were pushed inside

the cell and the heavy door bolted behind them. AMOS had been taken away immediately on their arrival at the palace, still locked inside his egg.

High on the wall was a monitor screen which had not been there before. A grey K'Thraa wearing a translator device at his neck was staring down at them from the screen. Once again Jonas was taking no chances – they would be watched constantly.

'Where are your children?' Marianne asked Sha'Rani.

'Gone,' the female K'Thraa replied. She, too, wore a translator. 'They were taken away when I was arrested on suspicion of helping you. They took my thoughtstone, too, so that I was not able to contact you again.'

She sat with her back to the monitor screen and spoke in a whisper so that the guard watching them could not overhear. Sha'Rani had a brood of young children, all of them hatched from eggs. Male K'Thraa greatly outnumbered females, and they fed the females with the drugs which ensured that their offspring became either rulers, warriors or slaves, depending on the colour of their skin.

Sha'Rani was an aristocrat, the brood-sister of Archmaster Ro'Sharok himself. But she, like all other female K'Thraa, hated the breeding programme. Once all three K'Thraa races had been not only equal but also less warlike. Sha'Rani had opposed the invasion of Earth and wanted nothing more than for the breeding programme to be stopped and for her race to live in harmony with human beings. This was why she had helped Hood and the others to escape when they had last been imprisoned by Jonas.

'Where have your children been taken?' Marianne asked her.

'All females and hatchlings are under protective custody. Most of them have been sent to Ro'Sharok's new citadel on Manhattan Island. He suspects all we females of plotting against him, and so they are all locked away and guarded.'

'How did they find out you had contacted us?'

'They were not sure I had. But I came under suspicion when you last escaped, and I was watched closely from then on. For a long time I did nothing to arouse their suspicions. But when I learned that Ro'Sharok was sending a fleet against your Worldship, I knew I must act and contact Hood through the stone. But other K'Thraa who wear such stones sensed my thoughts and that they were being transmitted into space.'

'Do you mean they could eavesdrop on you?'

'No, they would not know exactly what I said, or to whom I was speaking. But they sensed my urgency and the fact that my message was sent over a great distance. This was enough to confirm their suspicions, and so I was arrested and put into this cell.'

'Did you tell them anything?' Will Redman asked.

'I told them nothing. But my silence was taken for guilt.'

Sha'Rani had been glancing at Hood as she spoke. He had not reacted on seeing her, nor had he said anything since they had been taken from *The White Swan*.

'Hood,' she said to him, 'I sense great grief in you. Has your invasion failed?'

'It's going well,' Hood said without enthusiasm. 'We were captured because someone betrayed us, but others will continue the fight. And I think they will win.'

'Then why do you have such a great sadness?'

But Hood simply shook his head, as if to say that he did not want to talk about it.

Marianne, however, was more forthcoming. She told Sha'Rani all about Hood's parents and Adair and Isabelle. Hood had still not recovered from the shock of the terrible thing which had been done to them; he felt as if all the fight had been knocked out of him.

Sha'Rani looked grave on hearing the story, while Will and Mac exchanged glances, as though wondering whether they should complete the tale by saying who had performed the executions. But Hood simply turned away from them all.

Marianne crouched beside him. 'Hood, you've got to snap out of this. We've still got everything to fight for.'

'Others have to do the fighting now. We're locked up here.'

'Being in prison hasn't stopped you from wanting to fight before.'

Hood simply shrugged.

'Looks like we'll have to appoint a new leader,' Will Redman said.

'True enough,' Big Mac agreed. 'What use is a commander who just sits on his rump and has nothing to say for himself?'

'He's like a bottle of lemonade that's gone flat.'

'Never thought I'd live to see the day. You wouldn't credit that it was the same man, would you?'

Will shook his head theatrically. 'A shadow of his former self.'

'Who's going to take charge then?' asked Mac. 'Me or you?'

They both glanced at Hood. He gave a thin smile but remained silent, knowing that they were trying to provoke him into action. He felt too weary and dispirited to react.

Now Mitch came up to him.

'I'm sorry,' Mitch said. 'It's my fault we got captured.'

'No,' said Hood. 'You've acquitted yourself very well, Mitch. You showed great bravery when we were fighting for our lives in space against *The Black Swan*. It was you who were responsible for bringing the ship down. You should feel proud of yourself.'

Mitch was basically a cheerful sort, and he immediately brightened, a gap-toothed smile spreading across his face.

'What about you?' Marianne said to Hood. 'Haven't you got a lot to be proud of? You've done more than anyone to help liberate Earth. You can't give up now.'

Hood was silent for a moment, staring up at the K'Thraa on the monitor screen. The alien was watching them without expression, the milky membranes flickering across his swollen eyes. Then, in his mind's eye, Hood once again saw the agonized faces of his parents, and he felt only despair.

'Just leave me alone,' he said.

12

For two hours, nothing further happened. Hood and the others made themselves as comfortable as they could on the dirty straw, and waited. Overhead, the K'Thraa guard continued to stare down, the only motion on his face being the flash of membranes over his eyes.

Then they heard a shuffling outside in the corridor, and they knew that guards were approaching. The door was unbolted, and AMOS was bundled into the cell before the door slammed shut again behind him.

AMOS had been freed from his silver egg, and he glided forward on his air-cushion. His chest panels had been ripped out and much of the microcircuitry inside smashed.

'What's happened to you?' Marianne asked him.

'I've had all my non-essential systems destroyed,' AMOS told her. 'Jonas is determined that I will present no threat to him.'

'If he's *that* worried,' said Will, 'then I don't see why he didn't just take a sledgehammer to you.'

'That's because he values me as an automated system,' AMOS replied as if offended by the suggestion. 'He says that once Leon's forces are defeated, he's going to convert me into his personal servant.'

'He tried to reprogramme you the last time we were on Earth,' said Will. 'And that didn't work.'

'Quite so. But this time he has managed to disarm

me effectively. I can be of no assistance to you in an offensive sense.'

AMOS paused, then extended one of his arms down to the floor. He scooped up a large handful of straw and raised it towards his head. By now, a circular hole had opened below his eyes which corresponded to his mouth. He stuffed the straw into it.

This operation was repeated several more times, an electronic rumbling coming from his insides. Then he made a sound like a burp.

'Do forgive me,' he said, 'but my energy levels are running very low.'

AMOS was capable of eating a variety of substances from sand to sewage. Built inside him was an internal synthesizer which broke down anything he 'ate' and generated the electrochemical energy which powered him.

'Now,' he said, 'where was I?'

'You were telling us that you'd been disarmed,' Mac reminded him.

'Ah, yes. But all is not entirely lost. Would you all kindly begin singing?'

'What?!' said Will.

In a quieter voice, AMOS said, 'I have important news to impart, but it would not be wise for us to be overheard.' AMOS swivelled his eyes upwards to indicate the K'Thraa guard on the monitor.

'What do you want us to sing?' Mitch asked.

'That does not matter in the slightest.'

'How about "Nobody likes me, everybody hates me, just 'cause I eat worms"?'

'Hardly dignified,' AMOS replied. 'But if you insist . . .'

'We're not singing that,' said Will.

'Why not?' asked Mitch.

'Well, for one thing, I don't know the words.'

'Then what do you suggest?' asked AMOS.

Will shook his head. 'This is ridiculous.'

'That is not a song with which I am familiar. But the choice is up to you.'

'That wasn't a song title, dome-brain! It was a comment!'

'Look,' said Marianne, 'why don't we just hum whatever tune comes into our heads. It doesn't matter if they're all different as long as they drown out the sound of AMOS's voice.'

'Excellent,' AMOS agreed. 'Please gather around me.'

'I still think this is ridiculous,' Will grumbled as they formed a circle around him.

'Let's just get on with it,' Marianne told him, 'before Jonas sends someone down to find out what's going on.'

They had been talking in low tones, and the K'Thraa guard on the monitor screen was leaning forward in his seat, as if trying to hear them. AMOS counted to three, and everyone started humming different tunes.

The result was a horrible drone, but it swamped even the guard's voice as he shouted: 'Be silent immediately!'

AMOS did not waste time in saying: 'I suspected Selen may have been the real traitor when she fainted on board *The White Swan* – or rather, pretended to faint. When I took her to the sick-bay, the instruments there indicated that she was not really unconscious at all, but faking it. My suspicions were immediately aroused. So I administered a whiff of anaesthetic gas to ensure that she *had* passed out. Then I manufactured a tiny phial of the same gas concentrated into a liquid form which I then hid in the belt-buckle of her tunic.'

The K'Thraa guard on the screen had now vanished, no doubt to summon other guards to the cell. Marianne and the others stopped humming, and Will said, 'So that's why you spent so long with her in the sick-bay.'

'I wanted to be sure that we had some means of neutralizing her if she did prove to be a traitor. If her belt-buckle receives a blow, the phial will shatter and the gas will be released. It will act over a short range within seconds and works just as well on K'Thraa.'

'Then what happened?' asked Will. 'Where did your plan go wrong? And why didn't you tell any of us that you suspected her?'

'There was no direct proof that she was a traitor, and I did not wish to make hasty accusations. Unlike some people.'

'It would have been better if you had, AMOS,' said Marianne.

'Yes,' AMOS agreed. 'I'm afraid I miscalculated on more than just that score. I also believed that I had administered enough gas to keep her asleep for several hours. She regained consciousness far sooner than I had anticipated.'

Will Redman, always suspicious of robots, was quick to rub in AMOS's mistake: 'Your trouble is that you think calculations can solve everything. But people aren't like machines – they're all different and you never know what to expect of them.'

'I have already admitted my error,' AMOS said with dignified hurt. 'Nevertheless, the phial remains hidden in Selen's belt, and is a potential weapon which we may be able to use to our advantage.'

Hood had been silent up to now, not even joining in the humming. But he seemed about to say something when there was a shuffling of feet outside and the door was hurriedly opened.

Jonas burst in with a crowd of armed K'Thraa.

'What's going on here?' he demanded.

'We were having a sing-song,' said Will.

Jonas swiped Will across the face with his arm so that he went reeling back. Then Jonas snatched a stub-gun from one of the K'Thraa.

Glaring at the others, he said, 'You will tell me what you have been plotting. Otherwise Redman dies.'

The stub-gun was pointed directly at Will's chest.

But at that moment they heard a crescendo of thudding sounds. Jonas glanced up in alarm. There was no mistaking the sounds of the explosions. The palace was being attacked.

Shouting orders to the guards, Jonas retreated hurriedly from the cells. The guards also withdrew, bolting the door behind them. Their footsteps receded down the corridor.

Will's lip was bleeding from Jonas's blow, but there was a smile on his face.

'I think,' he said, 'that the cavalry have just arrived.'

For the next hour or so, Hood and the others listened to the dull thuds of explosions as the battle raged outside. The walls of their cell were thick, shutting out any other sounds. But there could be no doubt that a major assault was taking place on Jonas's bastion of power.

Soon, they heard K'Thraa approaching their cell once more. The door was opened and they were ordered out.

Under heavy guard they were marched up the stairway. AMOS, forced to move in jerky leaps from step to step, protested that his energy reserves were being drained, but the K'Thraa took no heed of him. They were hurried down a long corridor to an elevator which rose up through the palace's central tower.

At the top of the tower was Jonas's command centre. A broad curving window looked out over the front grounds of the palace, and both Jonas and Hi'Veshezz were standing at the window, staring out.

Ringed by guards, Hood and the others were pushed and prodded forward. Jonas, intent on the battle below, did not immediately notice them.

The prisoners gazed out through the window. Two concentric walls had been built around the front of the palace, and the first had already been breached by the human army who were swarming like a horde of ants through the snow.

Among the army were ground troopers in snow-suits – evidence that Leon had finally shattered the K'Thraa armada in space and was now landing troops all over the globe. But many of the attackers were dressed in rough clothing made from rags and strips of canvas; they carried crude weapons such as makeshift spears and bows-and-arrows. They were obviously slaveworkers from the K'Thraa plantations who had risen up and joined the liberating army to overthrow their former masters.

The alien defenders of the palace were already in retreat. Their desperation was obvious, for they were ordering groups of green K'Thraa into the forefront of the battle. The slave aliens were unable to refuse the orders, but they were not warriors and their short black tunics gave them little protection against the cold. As they moved sluggishly forward, they were easily shot down by the attackers.

Overhead, several manta-shaped K'Thraa scoutships were blasting away at the human army with the energy cannons in their bellies. But Leon's ground troops carried rocket-firing mortars and a scoutship was hit by one even as Hood watched. It shuddered for a moment in the air before bursting apart. Elsewhere, sonic grenades were being hurled into the cannon towers in the walls, with devastating effect.

Now the second wall was breached, and the attackers poured into the palace grounds. Jonas spun around with alarm, and only now did he become aware of the presence of Hood and the others.

'You've had it,' Will said to him. 'You're being overrun.'

'A temporary set-back,' Jonas said defiantly. 'Do not think that it will mean your rescue. I'll have you executed before I'll allow you to fall into the hands of those rebels. But there is no need for that. Arrangements have already been made to take us to safety.'

Hi'Veshezz was spitting orders to his soldiers.

Suddenly an explosion shattered the curving window, broken glass raining in on them. Hurriedly now, Hood and the others were frogmarched out of the command centre to the rear of the tower. Broad doors led out on to a landing platform for transporters and scoutships.

Sitting on the platform was *The White Swan*.

'We had the ship repaired,' Jonas told them, and they saw that the damaged section of the wing had been replaced. The new wing-tip was black, and it had obviously come from *The Black Swan*.

'We're taking you to the safest place on Earth,' Jonas told them. 'Ro'Sharok's fortress on Manhattan Island.'

An explosion nearby tore a chunk out of a concrete wall, scattering rubble across the landing strip. They were hurried on board. Jonas, determined that they should be kept in his sight at all times, ordered them to be taken to the bridge under heavy guard. There they found Selen at the controls of the ship.

She had discarded her blue-and-white tunic and was now wearing a flowing robe in Jonas's colours of crimson and indigo. The robe was secured at her waist by a thin silver chain. There was no sign of her belt, and it was clear that AMOS's plan had failed.

'I want them tied up securely,' Jonas told the K'Thraa.

Strong ropes were fetched and bound to their wrists before they were yoked together with a single long piece of rope. Even AMOS was not excepted from this, his golden hands being tightly tied together. Nor was Sha'Rani, who was tethered to

Hood at the end of the line. Armed guards continued to flank them on both sides to ensure that they made no false moves.

Hi'Veshezz shuffled over to Sha'Rani.

'Well, Mother,' he said, 'your days are numbered now. Ro'Sharok has certain proof of your treachery, and you will not live much longer.'

He spoke scornfully, without any pity whatsoever. Sha'Rani maintained a dignified silence.

'Have you nothing to say for yourself?'

There was no reply. Hi'Veshezz gave a harsh laugh and turned away.

Human troops now began pouring over one of the walls surrounding the landing platform. But the battlecruiser's hatches had been sealed, and Jonas ordered an immediate take-off. While he was occupied with ensuring his safety, Marianne turned to Sha'Rani and whispered, 'Hi'Veshezz is your son?'

'An older son whom I hatched over twenty of your years ago.'

'And Vu'Kashu was his father?'

Vu'Kashu was a Highmaster whom Marianne herself had killed on a previous mission when they were fighting for their lives. He had always treated Sha'Rani coldly, and she had not regretted his passing.

'Yes,' she replied. 'My son is a stranger to me, just as my husband was.'

'Why isn't he named after either of you?' asked Will.

'That is a human custom. We name our hatchlings according to what we see when they are first born. Hi'Veshezz means *A Shadow on the Ground*. My

110

own name is *Bright Cloud*, while Ro'Sharok is *A Stone Thrown by a Child*.'

It was a strange name for an emperor and only demonstrated how little they really knew about the K'Thraa. For a moment there was silence, and then Marianne said, 'It must be hard for you to have your son show such hatred towards you.'

'Some hardships are less difficult to bear than others.'

This was an odd reply, but there was no opportunity to pursue it, for one of the guards ordered them to be silent. Needle-gun darts were hitting the flanks of *The White Swan*, but just then Selen activated the main drive.

Within a matter of seconds, the battlecruiser was rising up over the palace. Hood and the others were grouped near a side viewport and so were able to see out. A furious battle was still taking place in the palace grounds, but on catching sight of *The White Swan* the human troops clustered in the snow raised their arms as if in greeting.

'They think Hood's come to help them finish off the attack,' Jonas said. 'I think we'll give them a surprise before we leave.'

He ordered Selen to fly *The White Swan* low over the palace grounds. Then he sat down in the co-pilot's seat, his finger poised on the button of the energy cannon in the ship's nose.

'It's rather a pity we have no torpedoes,' he remarked as they closed in on the human troops below. 'But the cannon will suffice.'

He opened fire, scarlet tracers flashing from the battlecruiser's nose across the snow-covered ground.

111

Many troops were cut down before *The White Swan* banked away.

'Excellent,' said Jonas. 'It would give me great pleasure to make another pass, and another, until all the renegades are slaughtered. But for safety's sake it is perhaps best not to linger. We shall proceed immediately to Manhattan Island.'

The battlecruiser sped away, leaving dozens of charred bodies on the ground below. Hood, aghast at what had happened, was staring grimly at Jonas. For the first time in hours he felt real anger.

13

In half an hour, they had crossed the Atlantic. On the way they sighted several starships, all of them vessels of Leon's fleet. This cheered Hood and the others, for it was a good sign that the fleet now had command of the skies. But *The White Swan* was not intercepted, and it was not hard to understand why. No one could have suspected that Hood and his crew had been captured by Jonas. If they spotted *The White Swan*, they doubtless assumed that it was still under Hood's command.

It was late morning New York time when they came in sight of Manhattan Island. Snow had been falling all the way across the Atlantic, and the island was a long strip of whiteness in the grey waters which surrounded it. All the buildings of New York City had been razed immediately after the invasion except for the Empire State Building. This, too, was now gone, and in its place stood a massive grey fortress like five granite snail-shells, grouped together in domino-fashion. Over this loomed a tower like a rearing serpent.

The skies above the island were clear of ships, and there was no sign of any attack taking place on land. Jonas ordered Selen to fly directly towards the serpent's head. At the same time he began to broadcast an identification code.

Presently a screen on the flight-panel lit up, showing a blue K'Thraa. Jonas identified himself and was quick to boast of his success in capturing not only Hood and his lieutenants but also *The White Swan*.

'You have done well,' the K'Thraa Highmaster told him. 'Ro'Sharok will immediately be informed of your success. Approach and prepare for landing.'

The serpent's head opened wide to reveal, in place of a forked tongue, a landing platform. Selen guided the battlecruiser down towards it. She was an experienced pilot, and had no difficulty in making a pinpoint landing at the centre of the platform.

The serpent's mouth closed over *The White Swan*, shutting it in. Both jaws were edged with huge zig-zag teeth which slotted together perfectly, blotting out the snow-filled afternoon.

Hood and the others were marched out of the ship and bundled towards the 'throat' of the serpent, where there was an elevator door.

'And so,' Jonas said to them, 'we come to the final reckoning.'

The elevator carried them down through the tower and kept dropping until they were far below ground level. Hood and the others emerged to find them-selves in a labyrinth of stone corridors and cave-like rooms. Below its covering of soil, Manhattan was solid rock. Jonas informed them that all the rooms had been hewn of the rock in the past year by teams of slave humans and green-skinned K'Thraa.

'This is the real nerve-centre of the K'Thraa empire,' he said. 'The palace above ground is just window-dressing.'

The network of corridors and rooms was lit by the reddish light which the K'Thraa favoured. Though the air was warm, the place looked bleak and gloomy. It was like being in catacombs where people were buried rather than lived.

Most of the rooms had slitted windows, and they were able to glance into them as they were marched along. Inside, female K'Thraa were huddled with their clusters of children, and guards watched over them. Blue-skinned mothers of the aristocratic caste mingled with grey- and green-skinned women, as did their children. Unlike the males, whose roles in society were rigidly divided, the females were on an equal footing. But they had no power and little status, the males valuing them only for the children they produced. It was little wonder that they opposed the invasion of Earth, Hood reflected, for they were just as oppressed as the human captives of the K'Thraa.

Sha'Rani kept glancing anxiously into each of the rooms, hoping for a glimpse of her own young. But they were hurried along the corridors by Jonas and the K'Thraa until finally they came to an arched doorway. Several guards flanked the door, though they hastened to open it as Jonas approached.

The room inside was large, and three of its bare stone walls were hung with purple and gold drapes. The fourth wall held a huge monitor screen which was surrounded by numerous other smaller screens. Hood had no doubt that they were in Ro'Sharok's command centre.

The room was surprisingly empty, but Hood and the others were marched forward and ordered to stand in the middle of a red circle which had been painted on the floor. Then the guards stepped back and Hi'Veshezz pressed a button on the control panel above the screens.

A cone of shimmering golden light descended from the ceiling immediately above, forming a wall around them. Hood stretched out a hand and found the wall as solid as stone.

'It's a force-shield,' Will Redman said. 'Just like the K'Thraa soldiers wear.'

'A security-cone,' Sha'Rani told him. 'They will take no further risks with us.'

Although the golden wall shimmered and flickered, it was also transparent so that they could see out. A door at the further end of the room now blossomed opened, and in shuffled a cluster of blue K'Thraa. And at the centre of them, sitting on a throne which hovered in the air, was Ro'Sharok.

The alien Archmaster glided up to the cone and regarded the prisoners inside. He was enormous, his throne being far larger than any ordinary K'Thraa chair. It looked as if it had been carved from stony wood.

Hi'Veshezz, Jonas, Selen and the guards immediately prostrated themselves on the Archmaster's appearance. Robes of purple and gold were wrapped around his body, there were rings on his fingers, and he wore a translator at his neck. He guided the throne by means of a control-panel on the right armrest. There was another panel on the other arm, holding just a single red button.

Ro'Sharok regarded them with eyes which were both lazy and malicious. Accustomed to wielding absolute power, he cared for nothing except maintaining his position through whatever means were necessary. He spoke first to Sha'Rani:

'So, my brood-sister, you tried to betray us after all.'

116

'I do not call it betrayal,' she responded. 'Tyrants must expect their subjects to resist them.'

'Resistance is futile. And you will have no further opportunity for treachery.'

Reaching into the folds of his robe, Ro'Sharok pulled out a long curving blade with a handle studded with red and green jewels.

'We will use this death-dagger to slit your throat,' he told Sha'Rani. 'Your executioner has already been appointed. He demanded the honour.'

Hi'Veshezz stepped forward, his head bowed and his arms outstretched. Ro'Sharok's mouth quivered in the K'Thraa version of a smile. He laid the death-dagger across the highmaster's open palms.

Straightening, Hi'Veshezz grasped the dagger in both his hands. He stared at his mother without pity.

'Do you wish me to strike her down now?' he asked Ro'Sharok.

Again the Archmaster's mouth quivered.

'Your hatchling is eager to end your existence,' he said to Sha'Rani. 'You should be proud of him. He is a true K'Thraa.'

Sha'Rani remained silent. Hi'Veshezz stroked the dagger's blade with his long fingers.

'The execution will be performed later,' Ro'Sharok said to him. 'We have other matters to attend to first.'

Now he turned his attention to Hood, staring at him for long moments before speaking.

'Again we have you,' he said at last, 'and this time there is no possibility of escape. This time I am going to make sure that you pay the most terrible price for your attacks against our empire.'

117

The milky membranes flashed across his eyes, and he drew in a hissing breath.

'Let me tell you what lies in store for you,' he went on. 'I am going to have your wife and friends tortured to the point of death – a very slow torture which you will be forced to witness. Then they will be turned into walking corpses so that they become our creatures, just as your parents did. Then *they* will be programmed to torture *you* – also with great slowness. We will keep you alive for as long as possible, and every moment will be as agonizing as we can possibly make it.'

Ro'Sharok ran his purple tongue across his lips as though relishing the thought. 'But first we are going to deal with this puny attack of yours – '

'Puny?' interrupted Will Redman. 'We've got you on the run!'

'That's a fact,' agreed Mac. 'This is going to be your last stand, you great big lump of blubber.'

Ro'Sharok pressed a button on the arm of his chair, and suddenly a jolt of agony surged through their bodies, causing all of them to slump to the floor. As the waves of pain slowly receded, Hood realized that for a second the floor beneath them had been electrified.

Ro'Sharok had already swivelled his throne towards the bank of screens.

'Ah,' he said, staring at the largest, 'I do believe that your fleet is massing for its attack now.'

The screen showed the cloud-filled skies above the palace. Out of the clouds were appearing the blue-and-white craft of Leon's fleet, flying in an arrowhead formation with the Chief Minister's star-shaped flagship at its head. Soon the sky was thick with ships.

Hood knew that Leon's fleet was assembling according to a previously arranged plan. They had decided that if they defeated the K'Thraa fleet in space, they would land ground troops all over the globe before concentrating their ships for an attack on Ro'Sharok's centre of government.

'Excellent,' Ro'Sharok said. 'Most of your ships are here, and so we will be able to destroy them in one fell swoop.'

He had pressed a button on the control panel below the screens, and now he said, 'Observe.'

His tentacled fingers pointed at one of the smaller screens which showed an exterior view of the upper fortress. The snail-like whirl of the central tower had begun to twist inwards on itself, at the same time opening out so that a hole grew at its centre. Immediately inside it was a long cylinder which looked like a black cannon. It pointed directly at the fleet.

'This is our gravity intensifier.' Ro'Sharok told them. 'It transmits a beam which acts on any metal object, causing its weight to increase a thousandfold. Within a matter of seconds, it will pull all the ships of your fleet out of the air and send them crashing to earth.'

Ro'Sharok's fingers were poised over the firing button. Just then, the clouds above Leon's fleet seemed to boil. Out of them loomed a massive sphere of black with silver and gold bands.

The Worldship.

It was clear that Professor Fitzwalter had finally succeeded in adapting a warp-drive for the Worldship so that it, too, had been able to jump across the gulf of space between Jupiter and Earth in seconds. But this was only to Ro'Sharok's greater pleasure.

'How splendid,' the Archmaster said. 'Now we can destroy not only the fleet but also their sanctuary. Then this rebellion will finally be crushed for ever.'

Hood looked at Marianne and the others. They were bound, imprisoned in a force-shield and surrounded by armed K'Thraa. There was absolutely nothing they could do.

Ro'Sharok pressed the button.

A beam of reddish light began to pour from the gravity intensifier, rapidly fanning out towards the Worldship and Leon's fleet. But at the same instant a similar beam of light, coloured gold, issued from the middle of the Worldship.

The two beams met head on, neutralizing one another. It was like watching two jets of different coloured water being fired together, the boundary between them rippling and changing but remaining in roughly the same place.

Then, as they stared, the gold beam from the Worldship slowly began to force the red beam back.

'No!' Ro'Sharok shouted with alarm. He frantically began pressing the firing button again, as if to feed more power into his beam.

But this had no effect whatsoever. With increasing strength, the red beam was forced back towards the end of the barrel. Everyone had gone still and silent in the command centre, all eyes – human and K'Thraa – fixed on the screen.

Irresistibly the golden beam edged closer and closer to the barrel. Hood felt the ground beginning to shudder under his feet.

The cannon burst apart.

The entire room was rocked with the power of the explosion, and the screens flickered momentarily before stabilizing. In one of them, Hood saw that the upper fortress had begun to disintegrate. He guessed that the gravity intensifier beam had not simply been neutralized by the beam from the Worldship, but reversed. And before it was destroyed it had magnified the mass of the fortress sufficiently to pull it apart.

Hood watched the five snail-like shell spires cave in, leaving only the serpent's-head tower standing. Dust mushroomed into the snow-filled air, and the others began cheering.

'You've had it now!' Mitch yelled at the Archmaster.

'Yeah,' echoed Will Redman. 'No matter what you do to us, you're finished.'

Ro'Sharok spun his chair around to face them. A froth of white spittle had gathered on his lips.

'You will not triumph, whatever happens.' He indicated the red button on the left armrest of his throne. 'This button will activate a series of anti-matter bombs which have been buried at the centre of every major continent of Earth. Your planet will be blasted apart. But not before I have first made my escape.'

The main screen showed hordes of spacesuited soldiers descending from Leon's fleet by means of jet packs. They were spilling out of the bellies of the ships, heading towards the ruined fortress.

Ro'Sharok pressed a button on his control panel, and the door at the far end of the room opened. The Highmasters were gathering around him, ready to make their escape, as were a now anxious Jonas and Selen.

Turning to Hi'Veshezz, the Archmaster said, 'Execute them all immediately!'

Then he scooted away, pursued by his retinue.

Hi'Veshezz did not hesitate. He stepped forward, the death-dagger at the ready. A dozen K'Thraa guards had been left behind with him, and they kept their stub-guns trained on the cone.

Hood watched the Archmaster and his followers vanish through the door, which folded shut behind them. He didn't mind dying, but he could not bear the thought that the Earth would be destroyed in its moment of liberation.

Hi'Veshezz did not switch off the force-shield cone but instead pressed a button on his belt-buckle which created another shield around himself. Being surrounded by an aura of energy, he was then able to step inside the cone.

The K'Thraa guards watched as he stepped in front of his mother and drew the death-dagger back. Then suddenly he dropped it, reached into folds of his tunic, and pulled out two needle-guns.

He tossed each of the guns to Will and Mac, then produced three more, which he thrust into the hands of Hood, Marianne and Mitch. Retrieving the death-dagger, he used it to sever their bonds, the blade flashing rapidly and expertly in his hands.

The guards, finally realizing that something was wrong, fired their stub-guns. But the blue-bolts splashed harmlessly off the cone. Now Hood and the others opened fire with their needle-guns.

Within seconds, all the K'Thraa guards lay dead. Hi'Veshezz stepped out of the cone and deactivated it. Hood and the others stared at him with amazement.

Marianne finally broke the silence: 'I don't understand.'

'He was on our side all the time,' Sha'Rani said. 'He had to pretend that he was going to execute me.'

'But how?' said Hood. 'How is it possible?'

'The breeding programme does not always produce perfect results,' Hi'Veshezz said, 'and I am not like other Highmasters. Like my mother, I hate our race's warlike ways. But it was necessary to pretend otherwise, for I would not have lasted long had my true sympathies been known to Ro'Sharok.'

'He's been my secret weapon,' Sha'Rani said. 'Even when I was imprisoned, he was able to contact your people and tell them about Ro'Sharok's gravity intensifier beam.'

Hood remembered the professor's coded message.

'*You* contacted the Worldship?' he said to Hi'Veshezz.

'I did more than that,' the young Highmaster replied. 'I sent details of how to construct a similar beam which would neutralize the weapon.'

Which explained why the professor had stayed behind aboard the Worldship after Leon's fleet had departed. He had been working not only on the warp-drive but also on the neutralizer beam.

'Why didn't you tell us he was on our side?' Hood asked Sha'Rani.

'It would have served no purpose,' she replied. 'We were all in captivity, and there was always the possibility that Ro'Sharok would use truth-drugs on you.'

'When you were brought to Jonas's palace,' Hi'Veshezz said, 'I realized that it was necessary to pretend to be hostile to you until the best moment arrived to try to free you.'

Will Redman was staring at the needle-gun in his hand. 'You've been carrying these around in your tunic ever since?'

'Ever since they were taken from you.'

The wall-screens showed various views of the underground fortress, and K'Thraa troopers were running about in panic. On several of the screens, Leon's ground troops could be seen, fighting their way down corridors. The K'Thraa's last citadel of power was being stormed. Hood knew that Leon's troops had been given strict instructions to leave all women and children unharmed.

'We've got to stop Ro'Sharok,' Hood said. 'What are his chances of getting out of here alive?'

'Very good,' Hi'Veshezz said. 'Especially if he intends to escape aboard *The White Swan*, as I'm sure he does.'

'Then let's make sure he doesn't!'

14

Sha'Rani took a stub-gun from a fallen K'Thraa, as did Hi'Veshezz, who also kept the death-dagger. The young Highmaster led the way out of the command centre, and they headed down a long corridor lit by blood-red wall lights. The corridor was silent and deserted, but the sound of explosions and gunfire could be heard elsewhere as Ro'Sharok's citadel was stormed by Leon's troops.

Hi'Veshezz had served in Ro'Sharok's court during the building of the underground fortress, and he knew his way through its tunnels by heart. He led the others away from the sounds of battle, knowing that the urgency of their mission would not permit them to be pinned down in any fighting. They had to stop Ro'Sharok, and that meant reaching the tower as swiftly as possible.

Everywhere K'Thraa women and children were huddled in rooms, peering out through the slitted windows with anxious eyes. Hood and the others did not attempt to release any of them. They would be safer where they were.

Turning the corner of a corridor which led to the tower's base, they encountered a group of K'Thraa soldiers. The aliens had activated their shimmering force-shields, but these were no protection against the needle-gun darts. Hood and the others, aware that they were fighting for the very life of their planet, unleashed salvoes of darts which quickly cut them down.

An elevator door at the base of the tower stood open. Hood and the others hurried inside and pressed the button to ascend.

The door closed, leaving them staring at an oval mirror on the wall under a dim red light. Swiftly the elevator began to carry them upwards. There was no indicator panel above the door, so it was impossible to tell how high they were rising. Hood was keenly aware of their vulnerability. If the elevator was sabotaged from above, they would plunge to their doom.

Silently they were carried further and further upwards. Hood peered into the mirror at the faces of the men and the women under his command. He could see their tension and their eagerness to put an end to Ro'Sharok's empire once and for all. Grimfaced, weapons poised, they waited.

Now there was a soft rush of air, and the elevator halted. Seconds later, the door hissed open and cold daylight flooded in.

They had reached the landing platform.

The serpent's head was raised, but *The White Swan* still sat on the floor of its 'mouth'. Ro'Sharok and his retinue were crouched behind one of the battlecruiser's wings, and they opened fire the instant the door opened.

Hi'Veshezz had deactivated his force-shield when they entered the elevator, and he was standing in front of the door. An energy bolt from a stub-gun hit him in the chest and he fell forward across the threshold.

Mitch frantically pressed the button to close the

126

door, but the Highmaster's body prevented it from shutting. Mac and Will dragged him inside while Hood and Marianne gave covering fire.

The door closed, sealing them off from the stub-gun fire. Sha'Rani knelt beside her fallen son, and she cradled his head in her arms. Milky membranes clouded his eyes, and he did not move.

'Is he dead?' Marianne asked gently.

'Yes,' Sha'Rani replied in a whisper.

Hood had never imagined that he could ever feel sorry for a male K'Thraa, but he did now. They all did. Sha'Rani had been the first to make them realize that not all K'Thraa were murderous tyrants, and her son had shown them that even males could be honourable. Hi'Veshezz had died as much for their cause as his own.

For a few moments Sha'Rani rocked her dead son in her arms. Then she laid him flat on the floor. Her eyes were wet with tears.

'There will be time for grief later,' she said. 'First we must stop Ro'Sharok.'

'What are we going to do?' asked Mitch. 'They've got us pinned down here.'

'I believe I have the answer,' AMOS said. 'We require a reflective shield of some sort. That mirror will do just nicely.'

'What are you proposing?' asked Hood.

'We take the mirror down from the wall. Then I shall hold it in front of me and lead the charge against Ro'Sharok and his followers. Any energy blasts will be deflected by the mirror. The rest of you will take cover behind me. With any luck, we should be able to storm their position.'

It sounded risky, but there was no alternative.

Big Mac stepped forward and gripped the edges of the mirror. With a powerful wrench, he detached it from its mountings.

'Before we go,' Sha'Rani said, 'I would like you to give me your thoughtstone.'

Hood was still wearing the stone around his neck. He wondered if she was withdrawing the gift she had made him.

'Why do you want it back?' he asked.

'Ro'Sharok wears one, too,' she replied. 'It is set in a ring on one of his fingers.'

Hood knew that it was possible for two K'Thraa wearing thoughtstones to link minds and even – if one of them entered a death-trance – to die together.

'I won't allow you to sacrifice yourself to destroy Ro'Sharok,' Hood said.

She looked down at Hi'Veshezz's body, then back at him. 'You must let me do whatever I think is necessary.'

'We attack first,' Hood insisted. 'Only at the last resort can you use the stone. That's my condition.'

'Very well,' she agreed.

He handed her the stone.

AMOS had by now picked up the mirror and was holding it in front of him. Everyone huddled behind it, their guns at the ready.

'I hope you know what you're doing,' Will Redman muttered to AMOS.

'If you have any better ideas,' AMOS responded, 'I would be quite happy to listen to them.'

'Just keep that mirror straight, otherwise we're all going to be fried.'

Hood turned to Mitch, whose hand was poised on the door-opening button.

'Ready?' he said.

'Ready,' Mitch replied. He punched the button.

The K'Thraa opened fire again immediately the door drew back. AMOS began gliding forward, the mirror held out like a shield. The blue bolts from the K'Thraa stub-guns hit the mirror's surface and were immediately deflected away. Hood and the others kept under cover, huddled beside AMOS as he led the advance.

Ro'Sharok and his group of Highmasters were still crouched behind the wing of *The White Swan*, though an airlock to the battle cruiser was now open nearby. Hood spotted Jonas and Selen on the edge of the group, and he suddenly saw that both were armed with needle-guns.

They fired clusters of darts at the mirror just as AMOS closed on the K'Thraa position. The mirror shattered, leaving AMOS and the others exposed. But the aliens were retreating towards the battle-cruiser, shielding Ro'Sharok, who was guiding his throne towards the airlock.

AMOS was hit by several stub-gun blasts, but he kept rolling forward, his bulbous body continuing to shield the others. A terrible electronic groaning began to issue from him as more energy bolts hit home, puncturing his metal skin. But still he continued on, while Hood and the others shot down the Highmasters as they tried to scramble into *The White Swan* after their emperor.

Jonas and Selen broke ranks and ran towards the tail of the battlecruiser. Marianne was at Hood's side, and she followed him as he went after the two traitorous humans.

'Go after Ro'Sharok,' Hood shouted to Will and the others, 'we'll get Jonas.'

The others raced forward towards the airlock, shooting down more of the Highmasters. Hood and Marianne hurried along the flank of the battle-cruiser, making no sound. Jonas and Selen had disappeared behind the ship's bulk and were equally silent.

Flurries of snow gusted in through the serpent's open jaws. As Hood and Marianne edged forward, there was a sudden movement near the tail, and both opened fire with their needle-guns. But they did not catch sight of their quarry , and all fell silent again.

Then, unexpectedly, Jonas called out: 'We surrender!'

Hood and Marianne reached the end of the ship. Jonas and Selen were standing immediately under the fan-shaped tail, their weapons gone and their hands resting on their heads.

Marianne moved towards them. The overhanging edge of the tail was only a few inches from the tops of their heads, and Hood suddenly realized their danger.

'No!' he called to Marianne, but it was already too late.

Jonas and Selen reached up and grabbed their needle-guns from where they had hidden them on the upper edge of the tail. Before either Hood or Marianne could do anything, they fired.

A dart from Jonas's pistol hit Marianne just below the shoulder-blade. She took a further halting step forward, then fell.

A cluster of darts flashed past Hood, narrowly

missing him. Jonas and Selen had already started running again. Marianne lay face up, her eyes closed, the snow-filled wind blowing her hair across her face.

Dead. She was dead.

Hood forced himself to look away from her. He dropped to one knee and took careful aim. Then he fired.

He had intended to unleash several clusters of darts which would cut down both Jonas and Selen. But only a handful of darts issued from the barrel of his pistol.

Selen was hit in the heart and she fell face-down on the landing strip, driving the dart deeper into her chest. Her body shuddered, then went still. Hood was already up by now and racing towards Jonas, who had reached the edge of the serpent's 'jaw'.

But Jonas had realized that Hood's needle-gun was empty of darts. Hood saw the scar on his right cheek writhe as he smiled and pointed the barrel of his own pistol at Hood. Then he fired.

Hood flung himself forward in a low dive so that the cluser of darts flew over him. Jonas was standing with his back to the tall teeth of the serpent's lower jaw. Hood's frantic dive sent him crashing into the governor, and both men landed in the cleft between two teeth, the upper halves of their bodies hanging over the edge of the serpent's mouth.

Jonas had managed to keep hold of his needle-gun, but Hood gripped his wrist and began wrestling with him. Far below lay the ruins of Ro'Sharok's fortress, the soldiers of Leon's army still pouring down towards it from the fleet above. Snow-thick

131

wind blasted through the serpent's jaw as Hood and Jonas wrestled on the edge of the precipice.

Both men were fighting for their lives, but Hood was enraged by the treachery which had cost Marianne her life and this gave him inhuman strength. With relentless force he squeezed Jonas's wrist to try to make him drop the needle-gun while pinning Jonas's other hand against his own body. Hood's left hand was now free, and he raised it above Jonas's head.

The wind drove snow into his face, but nothing could cool his rage. He brought his fist down hard against Jonas's jaw, and the governor's head slumped back, his eyes rolling up in their sockets.

Hood staggered back, steamy breath billowing from his mouth. Then, before he could even register his victory, Jonas suddenly lurched upright.

Blood was trickling from his mouth, but he had only pretended to be knocked out.

'Fooled again,' he said to Hood, smiling and raising his needle-gun. 'I always knew you'd never get the better of me, Hood. That was your last mistake.'

The pistol was levelled on Hood's chest, and Hood braced himself for death. He heard the sharp hiss of the needle-gun being fired, but no dart hit him. Instead it was Jonas who staggered back, and Hood saw the dart which had hit him in the centre of the neck.

He spun around. Marianne, wounded in the shoulder-blade but undoubtedly alive, had managed to crawl to her feet and pursue them. It was she who had fired the dart.

Jonas's mouth opened and closed several times,

but no sounds came out. He teetered back a few more steps, then overbalanced and fell through the cleft between two of the serpent's teeth, vanishing out of sight. He did not even scream as he plunged to his death hundreds of metres below.

Hood raced over to Marianne. Her jumpsuit was soaked with blood at the shoulder, and the dart still stuck out of the wound.

'I thought you were dead,' Hood began.

Marianne was in no mood for sympathy or congratulations. 'Hood, we've still got to stop Ro'Sharok.'

Already she was hurrying towards the ship. Hood went after her.

'Are you sure you're all right?' he asked anxiously.

'I feel terrible, but I'm not going to stop now.'

'We have to get that dart out of your shoulder.'

'Unless we stop Ro'Sharok, it won't make any difference. We'll all be blown to smithereens.'

Hood took her point. They hurried towards the ship's airlock. All around them lay the dead bodies of K'Thraa Highmasters – and AMOS. He was lying on his back, his ruptured belly pointing to the sky. Silver lids had closed over his eyes.

They had no time to mourn him. Creeping through the airlock, they found the long corridor which led to the bridge empty. But from its furthest end came the sound of gunfire.

Will, Mac and Sha'Rani were pinned down in the doorway to the bridge by the desperate stub-gun fire of the few remaining Highmasters. Ro'Sharok could not be seen.

'Jonas and Selen are dead,' Hood told the others

as he crouched down beside them. 'Where's Ro'Sharok?'

'Hiding behind an instrument bank,' said Will. He looked grim.

They all saw Marianne's wound as she slumped against the gangway wall. In response to their concerned glances, she said, 'I'm all right. Let's finish this off.'

'That could be a problem,' said Will. 'We're all out of darts.'

Sha'Rani was still carrying her stub-gun, but the K'Thraa Highmasters had activated their force-shields to protect themselves against such energy weapons.

Marianne checked the magazine in her own pistol.

'I've only got one dart left,' she announced.

The Highmasters had positioned themselves around the bridge so that they could fire at the doorway from any angle. To try to burst into the bridge would be suicidal.

'Where's Mitch?' Hood asked the others, suddenly fearing the worst.

'He claims he has an idea,' Mac said, 'though he wouldn't say what it was. He went off down one of the gangways a few minutes ago.'

At that moment Mitch appeared, a silver shoulderbag slung across his chest. He gave them all a gap-toothed grin.

'I went to look for some magazines for the needle-guns,' he told them. 'Instead I found these.'

Delving into the bag, he produced several golden eggs.

Sonic grenades.

They wasted no time. Each of them took a grenade and pulled out the pin at the same instant. Then they rolled the grenades at different directions into the bridge.

Seconds later, the grenades exploded silently. The K'Thraa Highmasters immediately fell, their weapons rolling out of their tentacled hands.

Hood and the others entered the bridge, expecting to find all the K'Thraa unconscious. But suddenly Ro'Sharok glided out of hiding.

He was still seated on his throne, and a transparent dome covered its top, sealing him in. His left hand remained poised over the red button, while his right hand punched out a code on the instrument panel. Suddenly they could hear his heavy, hissing breaths.

The dome was obviously impervious to sound and so had protected him from the sonic grenade blasts. But he had opened a communications channel, and now he spoke:

'So the battle is ended and you have triumphed. But it will be a futile victory. Now I shall destroy your whole world.'

'If you press that button,' Hood said, 'you'll die as well.'

'There is nothing further to live for. We K'Thraa are a race who believe in conquest or death. You are our enemy, and I cannot permit you to survive. Now you, and every other person on your planet, will join me in oblivion.'

Ro'Sharok's fingers descended towards the red button. Then they halted, quivering. The Archmaster looked up with alarm, staring at Sha'Rani.

Sha'Rani had dropped her stub-gun and put both

135

hands over the thoughtstone at her neck. Her eyes were closed and she was obviously concentrating hard – concentrating on preventing Ro'Sharok from pressing the button by the sheer power of her mind.

Ro'Sharok began to struggle, his breathing growing faster and his hand trembling more rapidly. But still he could not bring it down to touch the button. Hood was amazed. He had no idea that the thoughtstones could be used by the aliens to control another person's actions.

'Quickly,' Sha'Rani gasped. 'Break the dome!'

Marianne had already raised her needle-gun. She looked weak from loss of blood, but she steadied herself and fired.

The dart struck home and the dome shattered, hurling Ro'Sharok from his throne. He attempted to rise, to crawl back to it. Acres of fat moved and trembled on his body as he slithered forward like a huge slug.

Sha'Rani moved with surprising swiftness. From the folds of her robe she had drawn the deathdagger which she had taken from her son. With two hands she raised it above the Archmaster as he hauled himself up towards the red button. She brought it down swiftly, burying the blade in his chest.

Ro'Sharok made a gagging sound deep in his throat. He tried to reach for the red button, but suddenly fell back, crashing to the floor of the bridge. A loud hissing sound poured out of his throat, and then his eyes closed forever.

For long moments no one moved. Hood stared at the others, scarcely able to believe that it was all over. Then suddenly Will Redman broke the spell by hurrying out of the bridge.

Sha'Rani was staring down at the dead body of Ro'Sharok.

'So my son is avenged,' she said softly, 'and now we K'Thraa are free from tyranny once more.'

Through the viewport, Hood noticed a blue-and-silver transporter landing nearby. He and the others hurried outside.

On the landing strip, Will Redman was crouched beside AMOS's broken body.

'I'm sorry,' Will was saying to the inert body of the robot. 'I'm sorry for all the rotten things I said about you.' His eyes were wet with emotion, and he swallowed hard. 'Now you're gone, I'm really going to miss you.'

'Gone?' came a faint but unmistakable voice. 'What do you mean 'gone'? I have merely suffered some extensive structural damage, but my programme is still intact. Be so good as to help me to a standing position.'

The lids had opened on AMOS's eyes, and Will was staring down at him with amazement.

'You cheated!' he said. 'You were only pretending to be dead!'

'"Dead" is a term which only applies to living organisms. And since I am an artificial construct – as you are always eager to remind me – then "death" is meaningless when applied to me. Though I must admit I do feel rather under the weather, and I appreciate your concern.'

There was a hint of teasing in his voice. Will scowled and said, 'Aw, shut up, you great big metal bag of wind.'

With Mac and Hood's help, they managed to stand AMOS upright. The transporter had now landed, and out of its hatchway stepped Leon and Professor Fitzwalter.

Both men raced forward, obviously delighted to see Hood and the others alive. It was their moment of triumph, a time for joy and relief and congratulations. But before the two men could reach them, Marianne teetered and collapsed on the landing strip.

15

The Worldship sat at the centre of the main runway of Heathrow Spaceport. A broad ramp led up to an entrance portal, and K'Thraa women were filing on board, their children at their sides.

A month had passed since the battle on Manhattan Island, and the liberation of Earth was finally complete. K'Thraa forces all over the globe had surrendered on learning of Ro'Sharok's death, and now the aliens were being sent to a new home on another world.

Sha'Rani stood with Hood, Leon and Professor Fitzwalter at the end of the runway. Her seven young children played innocently around her feet, examining the dandelions which were flowering at the edge of the runway as if they had never seen such plants before. They had been found safe in one of the stone chambers of Ro'Sharok's citadel after the battle was over.

Hood watched the young K'Thraa in play, their alien faces filled with innocent mischief. All were males, and once they had been fated to grow up into ruthless overlords. But no longer. The professor and his teams of scientists had developed a hormone treatment which reversed the effects of the breeding programme so that all K'Thraa from now on would be freed from the compulsion to make war and destroy.

But there was a price to be paid. The K'Thraa

had invaded Earth and ruthlessly destroyed its cities and many of its people. And so they were being exiled – but to a planet where they would be able to survive.

'It won't be easy for your people on Venus,' Hood said to Sha'Rani. It was he who had suggested the planet as a new home for the K'Thraa, and Leon and the rest of the council had agreed to transport the aliens there. 'There are no buildings, no crops – nothing. You'll have to start from scratch.'

'It is necessary,' she replied. 'We have to pay a price for our aggressiveness.'

'We'll ensure that you're sent sufficient food,' said Leon, 'until the crops you plant have time to grow.'

'And the solar mirror's already in orbit,' said the professor. 'It will make Venus seem more like your old homeworld.'

The mirror was not needed to heat up the planet, for it was already hot enough. But it would filter the sunlight and turn it red so that it resembled the light of their parent sun, Betelgeuse.

'We are grateful,' Sha'Rani said. 'You owed us nothing, and yet you have given us not only our lives but also a new world to make our own.'

Leon grinned under his beard. 'Perhaps your people will elect you as their new ruler.'

'If they did,' Sha'Rani said seriously, 'I would refuse it. My people have had enough of rulers who abuse their power. I think it is time we learned to work together, as equals.'

One of the terms of the K'Thraa settlement on Venus was that they would not be allowed to have spacecraft of any sort for fifty years, until they had proved they had changed their ways. This condition

140

had been accepted without argument. And soon Sha'Rani would be joining the rest of her people aboard the Worldship, which would carry them to their new home.

'Tell me something,' Hood said to her, 'how did you manage to use the thoughtstone to stop Ro'Sharok from pressing the red button? I'd assumed they could only be used for telepathic communication.'

'In most cases you would be right,' she replied. 'But you forget that Ro'Sharok and I were hatchlings from the same brood.'

'What difference does that make?'

'Brood-brothers and sisters have a special bond, and their minds are more easily opened to one another. And if one is powerful or determined enough, then it can use a thoughtstone link to impose its will on the other for a short time.'

'You were certainly determined,' Hood said.

'Ro'Sharok had caused the death of my son, and I wished to be avenged. It would have been possible for me to kill him by entering a death-trance when we were linked through the stones. But then, of course, both of us would have died. So, for the sake of my other children, I preferred to use the death-dagger instead.'

Sha'Rani's children were now standing on a stretch of grass, watching the approach of five familiar figures from the control tower nearby.

'We'll be needing a K'Thraa embassy here on Earth,' Leon said, 'to ensure that your people's interests are looked after.'

'We'll have it specially built so that the conditions inside are right for your staff,' the professor added.

141

'And we want you to be the ambassador,' the professor added.

Sha'Rani stared at all of them in turn.

'I am honoured,' she said, 'but I must refuse. My place is with my people and my children. I want them to grow up on a world which they can call their own.'

At this point they heard high-pitched squeals from Sha'Rani's brood which indicated excitement. Mixed in with these sounds were very human shouts.

On a stretch of grass nearby, Sha'Rani's children were being taught to play soccer by Will Redman, Mitch, Big Mac and AMOS. Marianne, her injured shoulder in a sling, was acting as referee.

The young K'Thraa outnumbered their human opponents by seven to four, but the game was new to them and they moved clumsily. Will Redman, however, was giving no quarter. Dressed in a new scarlet coat and black three-cornered hat, he was racing around after the ball as if his life depended on it.

But Mac, Mitch and AMOS were showing more sportsmanship. They deliberately kept getting in Will's way to prevent him from scoring goals. AMOS, in particular, kept colliding with him as if by accident. He had been completely repaired, and his rounded body shone under the sunlight as he glided straight into Redman, knocking him to the ground.

Will glared up at him. 'You did that on purpose, you chromium-plated oaf!'

'I am still having teething troubles with my new stabilizers,' AMOS informed him. 'It was an unfortunate accident.'

'Unfortunate, my foot!' Will looked up at Marianne. 'Why haven't you blown the whistle for a foul?'

'I can hardly blow for a foul,' she told him, 'when AMOS is on your side.'

Meanwhile the play was continuing. One of Sha'Rani's sons kicked the ball towards the goal. It ricocheted off Mitch's foot, then trickled between Mac's legs across the goal-line.

'Well now,' said Mac, 'there's a drop of bad luck. An own-goal.'

Will sprang to his feet. 'You're all against me! It's a conspiracy!'

'Perhaps you would prefer to play chess,' said AMOS. 'Our score now is sixty-eight victories to zero in my favour.'

'We drew one game,' Will said instantly.

'Only because you knocked all the pieces off the board as I was about to checkmate you.'

'That was an accident.'

'You swept the pieces off the board with your hand.'

'I was trying to swat a fly.'

'There were no flies in the room. I would have been aware of them.'

'Your trouble is you're a know-all.'

'And your trouble is that you're jealous of my superior abilities.'

'Ah, go soak your solenoids.'

'The very fact that you always resort to personal abuse proves my point.'

The others were standing around, listening to the argument with patient smiles.

'You humans are strange,' Sha'Rani remarked.

'You show great bravery and honour in fighting for a just cause, and yet you squabble over trifles. I do not think I will ever truly understand you.'

Keeping the peace is harder work than making war, Hood thought. He stared out over the grassy fields between the runways. There was a whole new world to be rebuilt out of the ashes of the old, and it was the greatest task that had yet faced the human race. But Hood had no doubt that the survivors of the invasion would rise to the challenge. Earth was free once more, and men and women were in control of their destinies again. They had fought hard to liberate their planet, and now they would rebuild its civilization. It would rise anew as a monument to all those who had sacrificed their lives for the cause. It would stand as living proof that they had not died in vain.